"I can't believe I'm hearing this. I thought this was a merchant bank...not a marriage bureau."

"It is a bank, and I am its chairman," Reid said calmly.

"You wouldn't be for much longer if your shareholders heard what you're suggesting. They'd think you were out of your mind. You can't *buy* a wife."

"It isn't the usual method of acquiring one," he agreed, going back to his chair. "But these are unusual circumstances. I have neither the time nor inclination to follow the traditional course. You are in urgent need of someone to straighten out the financial shambles you find yourself in. If you agree to marry me, your mother won't have to move and you won't have to worry about her future. I'll take care of that. Think it over, Francesca. When you've had time to assess it, I think you'll agree it's an eminently sensible plan."

Dear Reader,

For twenty years, with my husband, usually in late spring and early fall, I've been crossing the range of mountains that separates France from Spain.

There are many different ways to cross the Pyrenees, from the sweeping curves of the *autopista* at the Mediterranean end to the narrower, more twisting minor roads in the central and eastern sections. We've tried most of them, including the route through the tiny principality of Andorra.

In between times, flying to London to meet my editor, often I've had an eagle's view of inaccessible valleys so high up that the snow never melts. It never ceases to amaze me that the long, uncomfortable, perilous journey of earlier centuries can now be accomplished in two hours by air. Even by car, it takes only a few days. We like to do it slowly, picnic-lunching in woods or by the banks of streams, spending the night at quiet country hotels.

On a recent journey, it struck me that it was time to write a book about these magical mountains that, if not as remote as they once were, still retain a feeling of tranquillity long lost in more populous areas.

A short time later I happened to catch a brief glimpse of a tall, striking man and a beautiful girl, both wearing shorts and walking boots. I shall never know who they were...and they will never know they were part of the inspiration for the story you're about to start reading.

I hope you enjoy it.

Anne Weale

The Bartered Bride
Anne Weale

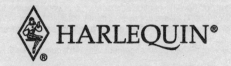

HARLEQUIN®

TORONTO • NEW YORK • LONDON
AMSTERDAM • PARIS • SYDNEY • HAMBURG
STOCKHOLM • ATHENS • TOKYO • MILAN • MADRID
PRAGUE • WARSAW • BUDAPEST • AUCKLAND

ISBN 0-373-03520-9

THE BARTERED BRIDE

First North American Publication 1998.

Copyright © 1998 by Anne Weale.

This edition published by arrangement with Harlequin Books S.A.

® and TM are trademarks of the publisher. Trademarks indicated with ® are registered in the United States Patent and Trademark Office, the Canadian Trade Marks Office and in other countries.

Printed in U.S.A.

CHAPTER ONE

EXPECTING him to be a middle-aged toad, Francesca was surprised when the man who rose from behind the large orderly desk was a tall dark thirtysomething, not precisely handsome but undeniably personable.

'Ms Turner...please sit down.' He gestured to the chair on the outer side of the desk and waited until she was seated before resuming his own seat.

She knew nothing about him, except that his name was Reid Kennard and he occupied a large office on the highest floor of a prestigious office block in the City.

This area of London was one of the world's great money markets. Judging by his discreetly luxurious surroundings, this man was one of the market's moguls.

To Fran, until very recently, money had been something she spent with careless extravagance on clothes for herself, presents for others and anything else she wanted. Now the supply had dried up. That was why she was here in the formidable presence of this well-built six-footer whose physique didn't match her mental image of a top-level financier.

All she knew about him was that Mr Preston, her late father's lawyer, had said that Reid Kennard wished to see her and might be able to help her and her mother out of their predicament.

Predicament being the understatement of the year, Fran thought wryly, leaning back in the comfortable leather chair and automatically crossing her legs, remembering a moment too late that this was a no-no in the books of advice on how to impress interviewers.

The movement caused Mr Kennard to shift the focus

of his cold grey gaze from her face to her shapely knees and then to her slender ankles.

Fran was accustomed to men admiring her legs furtively or openly according to temperament. Reid Kennard belonged to the latter group, but whether his frank appraisal was appreciative, critical or indifferent it was impossible to tell. He had the most deadpan expression she had ever come across. It made her nervous. She wasn't used to being nervous. She didn't like it.

The appraisal didn't last long, perhaps not more than three seconds. Leaning forward, his forearms resting on the edge of the desk and his long-fingered hands loosely clasped, he returned his gaze to her face.

'You're in trouble, I hear.'

Lacking any regional or social accent, his voice gave no clue to his background. Self-assured and brisk, it was a voice she could imagine giving decisive orders people would jump to obey.

Had she met him in surroundings not indicative of his occupation, and been asked to guess it, she would have surmised that he held a senior rank in one of the special units of crack fighting men called to the world's trouble spots when drastic action was the only solution. He had an air of contained physical power. A man of action rather than a desk-bound number-cruncher.

'Yes,' she agreed, 'we are. Since my father's death, my mother and I have discovered that instead of being comfortably off we're extremely hard up…virtually penniless.'

'Not penniless,' he said dryly. 'The watch you're wearing would pay the grocery bills of an average family for several months.'

'I shan't be wearing it much longer.' She looked down at the stylish Cartier watch her parents had given her for her eighteenth birthday. 'But I don't mind that. I can cope with the change in our circumstances. It's my mother I'm worried about. She's not young. She has never worked. She—'

He interrupted her. 'Nor have you, I understand. The press describe you as a playgirl.'

'The press puts labels on everyone...not always accurate. It's true I've never had a job. There was no point. My father was rich...so we thought. I wasn't brainy enough to train for one of the professions. I don't have any special bent. The most useful thing I could do was help to keep other people employed, not take a routine job someone else needed.'

'You don't have to justify your butterfly existence to me, Ms Turner. But without any work-experience, you're not going to find it easy to start supporting yourself, particularly not at the level you're accustomed to.'

'Presumably you didn't ask me here to tell me what I already know,' she replied, with a flash of irritation.

There was something about his manner that put her back up. He hadn't smiled when he greeted her. Beyond standing up when she was shown in by his secretary, he hadn't done anything to put her at ease.

'Why *did* you send for me?'

Rising, he picked up a file lying on the top of his desk. He walked round to hand it to her. 'Have a look through that.' He strolled away to a window looking out on a vista of rooftops. He stood with his hands behind him, the right hand clasping the left wrist.

The file held plastic pockets containing illustrations taken from magazines and the glossier kind of catalogue. Mostly they showed pieces of sculpture, paintings and other *objets d'art*. There were also several photographs of horses, an aerial view of an island off Scotland and a picture of a small French château.

Half turning from the window, he said, 'They're all things that caught my eye over the last few years. Some of them are now mine. I'm in the fortunate position of being able to indulge my acquisitive impulses…as I expect you did before your father died.'

'Not on this scale,' said Fran. She couldn't see where this was leading.

As she glanced enquiringly at him, Reid Kennard returned to his desk, resting one long hard thigh along the edge of its polished surface and folding his arms across his chest.

'There's one picture in there you'll recognise. Carry on looking.'

Intrigued, she obeyed, turning the pages more rapidly than before. Suddenly, with an indrawn breath of surprise and puzzlement, she stopped. She hadn't expected to see a photograph of herself.

It had been taken at a party for socialites. She was wearing a figure-hugging dress of black crushed velvet and showing a lot of sun-tanned cleavage, having recently returned from a winter holiday in the Caribbean.

'What am I doing here?' she demanded, baffled.

'You, I hope, are going to be my next major acquisition, Ms Turner.' For the first time a hint of amusement showed in the hard steel-grey eyes and flickered at the corners of his wide, chiselled mouth.

Inconsequently, it struck her that his mouth was at variance with the rest of his features. It was the mouth of a sensualist in the face of a man who otherwise gave the impression of being supremely self-disciplined.

But it was the meaning of his extraordinary statement, rather than the contradiction between his mouth and his eyes that preoccupied her at the moment.

'What do you mean?' she said warily.

'I need a wife. You need financial support. Do you understand the word fortuitous?'

'Of course I do,' she retorted, her long-lashed green eyes sparkling with annoyance at the implied aspersion on her intelligence.

It was true she had been considered a dunce by most

of her teachers and had never done well in examinations. But that was because she hadn't been interested in the things they wanted her to learn...grammar, maths, physics and incredibly tedious bits of history, all of them taught in a way guaranteed to send most normal teenagers—particularly the sort of restless, hyperactive teenager she had been—into a trance of boredom.

She said, 'It means happening by chance...especially by a lucky chance. But I can't see anything lucky about my father dying of a massive coronary in his middle fifties with his business on the rocks and his wife destitute,' she added coldly.

Matching her coldness, he said, 'In my experience, most people make their own luck. Your father's lifestyle wasn't conducive to a long healthy life. As a businessman, he took too many risks for a man with responsibilities.'

'Did you have dealings with him?'

She knew next to nothing about her father's business life. Since her late teens he had spent little time with his family. It was years since he and her mother had shared a bedroom. Fran knew there had been other women.

'Not directly. But after seeing that picture, I made a point of finding out more about you. I was on the point of making contact when your father died and I put the matter on hold. In the light of subsequent events, I've adapted my original plan to deal with things more expeditiously. If my information is correct, you have no relationships with men in train at the present time?'

'How did you find that out?'

He said coolly, 'I had you investigated...a reasonable precaution in the circumstances. Marriage is a very important contract. When people are buying a house, they have searches made by surveyors and lawyers. I had you checked out, very discreetly, by a private detective. You may want to run a similar check on me. For the time being my secretary has prepared a file which will give you most of the information you need.'

Retrieving the file she was holding, he placed another slimmer folder on the edge of the desk in front of her.

'I can't believe I'm hearing this. I thought this was a merchant bank…not a marriage bureau.'

Fran's eyes were both baffled and angry. He didn't look like a crazy person. In his expensive suit and diagonally striped silk tie—perhaps the emblem of one of those old boys' networks which still wielded so much influence—he looked eminently sane and sensible. But he must be out of his head to believe he could buy a wife as casually and easily as everything else in the file he was putting away in a drawer.

'It is a bank and I am its chairman,' he said calmly.

'You wouldn't be for much longer if your shareholders heard what you're suggesting. They'd think you were out of your mind. You can't *buy* a wife.'

'It isn't the usual method of acquiring one,' he agreed, going back to his chair. 'But these are unusual circumstances. I have neither the time nor inclination to follow the traditional course. You are in urgent need of someone to straighten out the financial shambles you find yourself in. If you agree to marry me, your mother won't have to move and you won't have to worry about her future. I'll take care of that. Think it over, Francesca. When you've had time to assess it, I think you'll agree it's an eminently sensible plan.'

For some reason his use of her first name detonated the anger which had been building inside her. Despite the red glints in her chestnut hair, it was rare for Fran to lose control of her temper. But she did now.

Jumping up, she said fiercely, 'I don't need to think it over. Nor would any sane person. I'm furious you've made me come here, thinking I'd hear something useful. This trip to London has been a complete waste of time.

I've a damned good mind to write to your board of directors and tell them they've got a nutcase in control.'

Without waiting for his reaction, she marched to the big double doors of solid mahogany and yanked one of them open. Glowering at the startled secretary at her desk in the outer sanctum, she slammed it resoundingly behind her and returned to the private lift which had brought her up to this rarefied level of the building.

'Is everything all right, Mr Kennard?'

His PA didn't know why he had sent for Francesca Turner, but she knew there could be no justification for the girl to emerge from his room scowling like one of the snake-haired Furies in classical mythology.

A conservative fiftysomething who had been promoted to PA while the late Sir Miles Kennard was chairman, Miss Jones knew enough about Ms Turner to conclude she was thoroughly spoilt.

Perhaps Mr Kennard had told her a few home truths. Although diplomacy was one of his many skills, when it was appropriate he could be outspoken, even ruthless. He was a much tougher man than his father. And needed to be. The world was a harsher place now than when she had joined the bank as a junior secretary almost thirty years ago.

'Everything's fine, Miss Jones, thank you.'

Although he was always formal, sometimes he gave her a smile which was far more rewarding than the casual use of her first name. That he should smile now surprised her. She had expected Ms Turner's ill-mannered exit from his presence to leave him in one of his forbidding moods.

As his visibly baffled PA withdrew, it crossed Reid's mind that Barbara Jones and Francesca Turner were about as dissimilar as any two women with roughly the same background could be.

The only child of middle-aged parents, Miss Jones had spent her adult life caring for them in their old age. She was the most selfless, reliable, deserving person he knew. The only rewards she could expect were the satisfaction of duty well done and a modestly comfortable pension.

Francesca represented the opposite extreme. It seemed likely she had never performed an unselfish act in her life. Unfairly, she had all the assets his PA lacked: a beautiful face and figure, a vibrant personality and a high degree of self-confidence, partly inborn and partly the result of an expensive élitest education.

Although Reid could usually predict how most people would react to any given circumstance, not having met Francesca he hadn't been sure how she would respond to his proposition. On the whole her spirited reaction had pleased him.

It showed that she was hot-tempered, impulsive and combative. At the same time it revealed that she wasn't a coward, willing to clutch at any straw to save herself from having to grapple with the gritty realities of switching from rich girl to poor girl.

From the moment she had entered the room, he had known that the shots in the social pages of the glossies hadn't given a false impression. In reality she was even more attractive than she looked in her photographs.

Although his main motive for marrying was not the customary one, it wasn't his plan to have the kind of relationship where physical pleasure was something found outside the marriage. The extra-marital liaisons engaged in by many of his peers were not on his own agenda. In his view there was no reason why a practical marriage shouldn't include good sex.

Taming that pretty firebrand until she ate out of his

hand was a challenge he hadn't foreseen but expected to enjoy.

Contrary to what she had angrily told Reid Kennard, Fran had another reason for coming to London: to pack all the personal belongings in her father's London *pied-à-terre*. This was now in the hands of an estate agent who expected to sell it quickly. Whatever price it fetched wouldn't help Fran and her mother. It would go towards paying off George Turner's numerous creditors.

The flat was near Marble Arch, part of a low-rise block built on the site of a large private mansion. All the trees had been carefully preserved, making the gardens surrounding the block seem an oasis of peaceful greenery in the heart of the noisy metropolis.

After her father bought the apartment, Fran had supervised the redecoration and chosen the furnishings. She had done the same at their home in the country. Her mother, a dedicated gardener, had no interest in interiors.

Occasionally Fran had toyed with the idea of taking a course in interior design and starting a business. But always something had happened to distract her. Anyway her most serious and important ambition had been to be Julian's wife.

As soon as she got back to the flat, she changed out of the businesslike black suit she had chosen for the interview with Reid Kennard. Under it she was wearing a white bodysuit, a flesh-coloured bra and sheer black pantyhose over micro-briefs. She stripped them off, stuffed her thick mane of hair into a plastic cap and took a long hot shower.

After putting on fresh underclothes and the apricot sweatshirt and jeans she had brought in her overnight case, she began to feel better, calmer, capable of reviewing the episode more rationally.

Coming back in the taxi, too upset to remember that taxis were a luxury she could no longer afford, she had found herself trembling with rage...and some other emotion not as easily defined. Now the most sensible course was to put the experience out of her mind. Forget it. Get on with the job in hand, clearing the flat of her father's things and her own.

Her mother had never come here. Daphne Turner disliked London. Big cities had nothing to offer her. Even the famous Chelsea Flower Show didn't appeal. She was a country person. Which was just as well because sometimes George Turner had entertained other women at the apartment.

Once, five years ago, Fran had arrived in London unexpectedly and found him in bed with an unknown woman at four in the afternoon. She could still remember the horrified looks on their faces when, thinking the flat was empty and puzzled by the strange noises coming from her father's bedroom, she had disturbed a scene deeply shocking to a seventeen-year-old virgin.

She had already guessed that her father was unfaithful, but to catch him in the act had been traumatic. Her affection for him, never as strong as her love for her mother, had turned to revulsion.

Her own experience of sex had been limited to a few kisses. By that age most of her friends had gone all the way, but Fran had been saving herself for Julian. She had known since she was fourteen that he was the love of her life and also that he wouldn't like it if she let other boys do more than kiss her.

The day his mother had told her he was engaged had been the worst day of Fran's life. She had always believed that he loved her but, because he was the son of Jack Wallace, her father's chauffeur, was keeping it under wraps until he had established himself.

Two months ago, she had been a guest at Julian's wedding. By the day she heard him say 'I do', she had pulled herself together enough to get through the service and the reception without showing the misery she felt.

A week later her father had died. Soon after that, when the truth about his business came out, her mother's world had caved in.

Recently, life had been a series of disasters. But that was the way it went. One damn thing after another. And it wasn't over yet. She had to find somewhere affordable for her mother to live and the means to support them both. A tall order.

She was on her way to the kitchen to make a cup of coffee when someone pressed the front-door buzzer. Answering it, Fran found a motorbike messenger outside.

'Ms Turner?'

'Yes.'

'Package for you. Would you sign for it, please?'

Fran wrote her name on the form and took the padded bag. There was nothing to indicate where it came from, only a plain white label with her name and address printed on it. Perhaps it was something she had ordered and forgotten about?

She closed the door and, walking back to the living room, pulled the tab that opened the bag and peered at the contents, immediately recognising the file Reid Kennard had said was a résumé of his life. Now there was a sheet of headed paper clipped to the cover.

Aiming at the sofa, Fran flung the package from her. Bloody cheek! Infuriating man! As soon as she'd had her coffee, she'd find some sticky tape and a label and send the file back, unstamped, with UNSOLICITED, UNWANTED BUMPH written large above the address.

She went to the kitchen, half filled the electric kettle and perched on a stool at the breakfast bar. Usually she drank herb tea, being on a more or less permanent health kick. But sometimes, on days like this, she allowed herself a shot of caffeine.

Postponing dealing with the package, she spent the next hour going through her father's wardrobe, making sure there was nothing in the pockets of his suits before she folded them. Rather than giving them to a charity shop, she hoped to sell them. The chaos he had left behind him made it essential to raise money in every way possible.

With the hanging cupboards empty, the next job was the drawers…but after another cup of coffee, or maybe a glass of white wine.

She opened a bottle of Muscadet and filled a glass. Instead of taking it back upstairs, she couldn't resist her curiosity about the letter that man Kennard had sent with the file.

Later she debated going to a movie to take her mind off her problems for a couple of hours. But there was still a lot to be done and she had already wasted half an hour reading the contents of the file.

She decided to phone for a pizza and concentrate on the job in hand. Some time during the evening she would telephone her mother. Mrs Turner didn't know about the interview with Kennard. Fran had felt it best not to mention it. She'd been trying to play down the financial side of their situation.

Her supper arrived sooner than she expected. But when she opened the door, it wasn't a pizza delivery man who stood outside. It was Reid Kennard.

Fran's friendly expression froze into a mask of dislike. 'What do you want?' she said curtly.

'I thought you might have calmed down a little by now.'

'I haven't…and I'm busy.'

She started to shut the door but he put a foot across the threshold and the flat of his hand on the door to hold it open.

She had never expected to hear herself saying, 'How dare you?' to anyone, but it was what sprang to her lips, followed by, 'Get out!'

'I'm not inside yet,' he said blandly. 'We have things to talk about. May I come in?'

'We have *nothing* to say to each other. You have no right to pester me like this. If you don't go away, I'll call the security man and have you thrown off the premises.'

'On what grounds?'

'Making a nuisance of yourself.'

Reid Kennard smiled, but it wasn't a kind or amused smile. It was the sort of expression she associated with sadists about to do something which would give them pleasure but cause excruciating pain to their victim.

'I think you're bluffing.'

He stepped into the hallway. To her chagrin, Fran let him. Not that she had much option. He was far too large and muscular for her to use physical means to deny him access. She had muscles of her own, but not in the same class as his.

He had looked a strong man in his office, but that might have been partly good tailoring. Now that he had changed out of his city suit into chinos and a dark blue cashmere sweater over a cotton shirt, it was clear that the breadth of his shoulders owed nothing to clever padding.

'This is outrageous,' she snapped, while instinctively backing away to avoid coming into contact with that tall and powerful male body as he closed the door.

'Don't pretend to be in a panic. You know perfectly well I'm not going to harm you.'

'How do I know that? You've already shown signs of derangement.'

'Not really. I'll admit to being unconventional. You'll get used to it.' He glanced round the hall and then, with a gesture at the open door of the living room, said, 'After you.'

Having no choice but to act on her threat or let him

speak his piece, Fran walked ahead of him. If he expected to be invited to sit down, he could think again.

Grinding her teeth, she saw that she had left the file on the low glass-topped table in front of the sofa. Even worse, it was open, proving she had looked through it.

But the first thing that caught his eye wasn't the file. It was the half-full glass of wine—her second—she had left by the telephone.

'A bad habit...drinking alone,' he remarked, with a sardonic glance at her hostile face.

'I don't as a rule. It's been a trying day. I'm not used to dealing with people who think they can trample roughshod over the rest of the world.' She folded her arms and glared at him. 'You have to be the most objectionable person I have ever met.'

'Because I want to marry you? Even if they don't wish to say yes, most women regard a proposal as a compliment.'

'Not when it comes from a stranger who regards women as chattels.'

'There are cultures where it's the custom for girls not even to see their husband's face until after the marriage ceremony. Marriage is a practical institution. It's because our culture ignores that that we have so many divorces. Wouldn't you rather stay married?'

'I'm not interested in marriage...certainly not to you.'

'Why not, if there's no one else in your life? Or did my investigator slip up there?'

At this point the buzzer sounded again. She saw him looking displeased by the interruption as she went to answer the door. This time it was the takeout delivery man. She took the box to the kitchen before paying him the money she had ready in her pocket.

Rejoining Kennard, she said pointedly, 'My supper's arrived. I'd like to eat it while it's still hot.'

Ignoring the hint, he said, 'You ought to keep your door chained until you see who your caller is.'

'Normally I do. It's only because I thought you were the man with the pizza that you were able to barge in.'

'That was lucky...for me.' He began to look round the room, taking in the colour scheme, the books and paintings, and the mirrors. Fran loved mirrors, especially antique ones. As a child, her favourite book had been a copy, inherited from her grandmother, of *Through the Looking-Glass*. Somehow the wrong-way-round view seen through a mirror always looked better than what was really there. She had often wished she could step through the frame of a mirror into a world where things were the same but different; her parents' marriage a happy one and herself a model pupil like her elder sister.

'Nice room. Who designed it?' asked Kennard.

No one had ever remarked on the way the room looked. She couldn't help feeling a slight sense of gratification that someone had finally noticed the effect she had spent a lot of time and thought achieving.

'Nobody well known,' she said. 'Please...I want to get on with my supper and I have to have everything packed by tomorrow afternoon. I really don't have time to talk...even if we had anything sensible to talk about.'

'A pizza's a poor sort of supper...especially if you're eating alone. Let me buy you a decent dinner and try to convince you that my plan makes a lot of sense. Then, if you like, I'll give you a hand with the packing.'

'Absolutely not! No way!' Fran said emphatically, but not with much hope he would accept her refusal.

He didn't. 'No to dinner, or no to help with the packing?'

'No to both...no to everything. Have another look through some magazines and pick out some other woman. I'm not for sale, Mr Kennard.'

'Do you like music?' he asked.

Disconcerted by the seemingly irrelevant question, she said, 'Some music...yes.'

'How do you feel about Smetana?'

'Never heard of him.' It was an exaggeration. She had heard the name but that was the limit of her knowledge.

'He was a Bohemian composer who lived in the last century. His most important work was done in Prague, helping to form a national opera. He had a nasty end…went deaf and died insane.'

'If I wanted to know about the lives of obscure composers I'd borrow a book from the library.'

'Is reading one of your pleasures?'

'Yes, as it happens it is, but—'

'That's good. It's one of mine and I have a large private library.'

Feeling her temper starting to simmer, Fran said impatiently, 'I shouldn't think it includes the kind of books I enjoy and if Smetana is one of your favourite composers your CDs would send me to sleep. I had enough of that stuff in musical appreciation sessions at school. I only like pop music.'

It wasn't true. Julian had taught her to share his love for classical music, but if Kennard thought she was what he would define as a Philistine so much the better. It might put him off this insane determination to marry her.

Not visibly deterred, he said, 'The reason I mentioned Smetana is because his most famous opera is called *The Bartered Bride*. Barter, the exchange of goods, was how people traded before money was invented. I'm not trying to buy you, Francesca. I'm proposing a trade-off…things I need for things you need. Are you sure you won't change your mind and come out to dinner?'

'Definitely not!'

'In that case I'll leave you to your pizza and take myself off for some Arbroath smokies at Scotts, or maybe their Loch Fyne smoked salmon.' As he mentioned two specialities of one of London's best restaurants, the hard eyes warmed with malicious amusement.

Could his private detective have found out that she adored fish and seafood?

On his way to the door, Kennard added, 'I'll call you in the morning. After you've slept on the idea, you may find it more appealing.'

'Thanks for the warning. I'll take the phone off the hook,' she snapped, as he let himself out.

CHAPTER TWO

SINCE Julian's wedding, Fran had had a lot of sleepless nights, prowling around in the small hours, tortured by thoughts of Julian making babies with Alice...babies which should have been hers.

All she had ever really wanted was to be Julian's wife and the mother of his children. Not the kind of ambition applauded by the teachers at the expensive boarding-school where she and her sister had been sent to learn to be 'ladies'.

That had been Gran's idea. Though Gran's own origins were humble, she was a tremendous snob and hadn't approved of her eighteen-year-old Daphne marrying a rough diamond like George Turner, even if he had gone on to make pots of money.

Gran wanted to see her granddaughters marrying men who were not only well off but also what she called well-spoken. To that end she had chivvied her son-in-law into sending the girls to one of the most exclusive schools in England. To Gran's disappointment, her eldest granddaughter, Shelley, had fallen in love with a young man who had once spent a summer working in her mother's garden. He now had his own plant nursery and was a contented man, but he didn't make a lot of money. John and Shelley couldn't afford to support her mother. With two small children and another on the way, they didn't even have a spare bedroom to offer her.

Had Gran known of Fran's secret passion for the chauffeur's son, she would have disapproved, at least until his achievements at university had signalled an impressive future.

The irony was that Gran would probably regard Reid Kennard as a wonderful catch. She didn't think much of love as a basis for wedlock. She wouldn't admit it under torture, but her granddaughters suspected there had been a metaphorical shotgun in the background of her wedding, and the marriage hadn't been happy.

In the morning Fran woke with a headache, the result of too little sleep and too much wine the night before. Staying up late, she had finished the bottle.

She spent the morning sorting out things in her bedroom and waiting for Reid Kennard's call. When the telephone remained silent, she should have been relieved. Instead she felt oddly uneasy.

What if he'd changed his mind? What if her animosity had made him have second thoughts? During his solitary dinner he might have decided he couldn't be bothered to wear down her opposition when there were plenty of women he could have for the asking.

The longer she considered this scenario, the more it seemed to Fran that she might have rejected in haste an opportunity she would live to regret turning down.

As things stood, all the future offered was relative penury for her mother and a dull job for herself. It wasn't an attractive prospect.

The trade-off Reid had suggested—suddenly she found herself thinking of him by his first name instead of his surname—would mean that if they were miserable, they would at least be miserable in comfort.

But what about her side of the trade-off: being the wife of a man she didn't love and who didn't love her?

Well, love, for long the first item on her private and personal wish list, had been crossed off the day Julian married Alice. So that brought it down to the question of whether she could face having sex with someone other than Julian in order to have some babies. They wouldn't have the father she had dreamed of, but any father had to be better than none.

Thinking about sex with Reid, Fran felt a strange sensation in the pit of her stomach. He had all the physical makings of a good lover; his aura of animal magnetism deriving from a great body, a sensual mouth, hands that looked strong enough to crush, but also capable of performing the most delicate and subtle caresses. Just thinking about the components of his disturbing personality sent strange little quivers through her.

Even though still a virgin, her innocence saved as a gift for her first and only love, Fran knew all the theory, knew what those frissons meant. She had recognised the passionate depths of her nature a long time ago. From the beginning of adolescence she had been excited and moved by amorous scenes in books and movies, recognising her capacity to feel the same fiery emotions as the women in the stories and on the screen.

But she had also had a strong streak of idealism. After falling in love with Julian, keeping herself inviolate for him had seemed more important than indulging her natural curiosity about what it felt like to do the things many of the girls in her class had experienced as soon as they were sixteen.

A lot of them were the over-indulged, under-disciplined children of broken marriages. During the holidays they had too much pin money and not enough supervision. Several girls she knew by sight hadn't completed their time at school. They had been expelled for serious misdemeanours ranging from night-time truancy to drugs.

Fortunately, although described as 'lazy', 'inattentive' and 'irresponsible' in her school reports, Fran had never been taken up by the group known to the serious-minded girls as The Decadents. The fact that she was reserving herself for Julian would have debarred her from that clique. Although far from being a teacher's pet, from

The Decadents' point of view Fran was one of the girls they called The Nuns.

She was thinking about her lack of sexual experience and wondering what conclusions the detective had drawn about her in that respect, when the telephone started to chirrup.

She forced herself not to grab it, letting it signal six times before she said coolly, 'Hello?'

'Good morning.'

If the distinctive voice at the other end of the line had mocked her about not leaving the phone off the hook, she would have cut the connection and dashed round the flat disconnecting all the extensions.

But Reid didn't refer to her parting shot. He said, 'I'd like to show you my library. Will you have lunch with me?'

She drew in her breath, knowing she was on the brink of one of the defining moments of her life.

'If you're worried about being alone with me, you needn't be,' Reid went on. 'My household is run by staff who are far too respectable to stay with any employer who doesn't live up to their standards. But even if that were not so, I've already made it clear my intentions are honourable.'

She could guess from the tone of his voice that there would be a sardonic quirk at the corner of his chiselled mouth.

'All right,' she said. 'What time and where?'

When he had rung off, she looked at the exclusive address she had jotted down on the notepad and wondered why she had relented.

Less than twenty-four hours ago she had stormed out of his office, convinced he was out of his mind. Now she was going to have lunch with him. Had she gone out of hers?

* * *

Before setting out for their lunch date, Fran reread the file Reid had sent her.

He was thirty-four, twelve years older than herself. A big age gap. It seemed likely that wasn't the only gulf between them.

Kennards, a merchant bank dealing with long-term loans for governments and institutions and advising on takeover bids, had been founded by his great-grandfather. The controlling influence had been retained by Thomas Kennard's descendants.

Unlike her father, Reid hadn't had to claw his way up from nothing. The facts in the file indicated that from birth he had been groomed for the position he occupied. But family influence couldn't have made him head boy at his public school if he'd lacked the qualities needed for that position, nor could it have gained him an impressive degree at one of England's most prestigious universities. He had to have a brilliant brain.

So why pick someone as unbrainy as me? Fran pondered uneasily. She knew she had other equally important qualities and had never wanted to exchange them for a superior intellect. But for a man like Reid deliberately to select a female who operated by instinct rather than logic seemed strange, not to say suspect.

He lived in a large house in one of the most select squares in the ultra-fashionable Royal Borough of Kensington. The butler opened the door to her and took her coat.

A man in his fifties, dressed in an ordinary dark suit with a discreet tie, he led her up a sweeping staircase, past a line of family portraits, to a large first-floor landing. As they reached it, Reid was descending the stairs from the floor above. She noticed his thick dark hair was damp and wondered why. It seemed an odd time of day to take a shower.

'You're admirably punctual,' he said, holding out his hand to her.

As they hadn't shaken hands the day before, it was her first experience of the firm clasp of his fingers. Then he took her lightly by the elbow to steer her across a rose and gold Aubusson carpet and through open double doors in an elegant drawing room with three tall windows overlooking the square.

Normally Fran would have swept an appreciative glance around the beautiful room, taking in some of the details. Instead she was overwhelmed by the strength of her reaction to their first physical contact.

'I nearly kept you waiting,' said Reid. 'I came back from the bank at eleven to go for a run in the park. As I was coming home I saw an old man on a bench who obviously needed medical attention. That held me up.'

'Do you run every day?'

'I try to. Are you a runner?'

Fran shook her head. 'I play tennis and ski. I don't do work-outs.'

He slanted an appraising glance at her figure. Today, in place of the black suit, she was wearing a designer outfit bought on a holiday in Italy. It consisted of a fine jersey-knit top in lilac, a waistcoat in violet, and a swirling chevron-striped skirt combining those colours with pink and pale pistachio-green. The audacious colour combination was perfect with Fran's dark red hair and green eyes.

'You look in good shape,' he remarked. 'But people in desk jobs like mine need some kind of fitness regime to stave off the bad effects of a sedentary lifestyle. Come and sit down. What would you like to drink before lunch?'

She remembered his remark about the wine she had been drinking when he forced his way in the previous evening. Was he one of those people who drank only mineral water and made everyone who didn't feel on a lower plane?

Fran had no intention of allowing him to intimidate her. 'A Campari and soda, please,' she said firmly.

Reid said to the butler, who had been following them at a discreet distance, 'A Campari for Ms Turner and my usual, please, Curtis.'

With a silent inclination of the head, the butler withdrew.

'Let's sit over here, shall we?' Reid steered her towards a group of comfortable chairs near one of the windows. 'Have you finished your packing?'

'Almost.'

Knowing that she wouldn't be able to sleep, she had worked on it till long past midnight. At half past nine this morning a dealer from whom she had bought a lot of the furnishings had come round to buy them back. Luckily Fran had paid for them out of her bank account. Although the money in it had come from her father, technically they were her property, not his. As soon as his business had been forced into receivership, everything George Turner had owned, including the family home, belonged to his business creditors. But the cash the dealer had handed her could go in her own pocket.

It wasn't much but it was better than nothing if, when Reid spelt out the terms of this trade-off marriage, she found that she couldn't accept them.

'What date is this house?' she asked, looking up at the elegant cornice around the ceiling and the two crystal chandeliers, their chains swathed with coral silk to match the festoons of silk cord and big coral tassels at the tops of the heavy cream curtains.

'Late eighteenth century. Are you interested in architecture?' He sounded faintly surprised.

'Sometimes.'

The butler came back with their drinks, hers a slightly more vivid red than the coral linen slipcovers on some of the sofas, Reid's colourless except for a twist of lemon floating among the ice cubes. It could be gin or vodka, or it could be straight mineral water.

Reid said, 'This was my grandparents' house. My paternal grandmother still lives here when she's not staying with her daughters. I moved here when my father died. We had been living in Oxfordshire and commuting by helicopter. For the time being I have an apartment on the top floor. But I thought you would feel more comfortable being entertained in the main part of the house,' he added, with a gleam of amusement.

After a slight pause, he added, 'I shall move out when I marry. The country is better for children...if their parents can choose where to live. Most people can't of course.'

'Where are you thinking of moving to?' Fran asked.

'I haven't decided.' His expression was enigmatic. 'Where would you choose to live, given a free choice?'

Fran considered the question. Once the answer would have been 'Wherever Julian wants to live'.

She said, 'Probably not in England. Ideally, I'd like more sun than we get in this country. I wouldn't mind living by the sea...or a lake would do as long as it had mountains round it. I'd like to look out on mountains...big ones with snow on top.'

He lifted an eyebrow. 'Sounds as if New Zealand would suit you.'

She shook her head. 'I'm sure it's a beautiful country but it's too far away from Europe. Have you been there?'

Reid nodded. 'The scenery's magnificent...when it's not raining. The South Island shares England's problem. Unreliable weather. Where have your travels taken you?'

'Mostly to holiday places...the Caribbean in winter...resorts round the Med in summer. My mother's a passionate gardener. She doesn't like travelling alone, even in a group. I've been on some garden tours with her...the south of France, Ireland, California. Where do you go for your holidays?'

'I used to go with my father who also liked someone with him. We went to Japan together and to other Pacific Rim countries. I travel a lot for the bank. For pleasure I usually go to France or Spain. Where would you like to go for our honeymoon?'

The question, tacked on to innocuous small talk, took her by surprise.

'I haven't agreed to marry you,' she said coldly.

'If you found the idea unthinkable, you wouldn't be here,' he said dryly. 'Let's be straight with each other, Francesca. I need you...you need me. It's a sensible, practical arrangement.'

She knew that at least the first part of what he said was true, but she wasn't about to admit it. Was it pride that made her reluctant to fall in with his plan too readily?

She said, 'I'm not clear why you've selected me.'

'You're very attractive...as I'm sure you're aware.'

'Is that all you want in a woman? An acceptable face and figure? Don't you care what I'm like inside?'

'I can make some intelligent guesses. People can't hide their characters,' he told her casually. 'Even in repose a face gives a lot of clues to its owner's temperament. Apart from yesterday's evidence that you have a short fuse, I haven't detected any characteristics I wouldn't like to live with.'

His arrogance took her breath away. In that moment of silent shock, she was struck by the thought it would be both a challenge and public service to bring this man down from his lofty pinnacle and convert him into an acceptably unassuming person.

But perhaps it was already too late. One of Gran's favourite sayings was, 'What's bred in the bone must come out in the flesh.'

Reid, with his long-boned thoroughbred physique and

his autocratic features, looked a descendant of genera-
tions of men who had felt themselves to be superior
beings and never experienced the doubts felt by ordinary
people.

In a different, more rough-hewn way, her father had
been the same. Probably, somewhere far back in Reid's
ancestry, there had been a man like her father: a rough-
diamond unscrupulous go-getter who had founded the
Kennard fortune.

Perhaps, if George Turner had married someone better
equipped to handle him than her quiet and easily cowed
mother, her father might have been saved from becoming an overbearing braggart.

Whether, at thirty-four, Reid's essential nature could
be modified was problematical. But it could be interesting to try.

She said, 'I don't find you as transparent as you seem
to find me. It takes me longer to make up my mind about
people.'

'You haven't had as much experience of summing up
people as I have.'

The butler reappeared. 'Luncheon is ready when you
are, sir.'

They ate in a smaller room with a view of a large garden,
an oasis of well-kept greenery in the heart of the city.
The surface of the round Regency breakfast table had
the gleaming patina resulting from nearly two centuries
of regular polishing. It reflected the colours and shapes
of the red-streaked white tulips arranged in what Fran
recognised as an antique tulip-pot, its many spouts designed to support the stems of flowers which had once
been costly status symbols.

The meal began with potted shrimps served with crisp
Melba toast, tiny green gherkins and a dryish white wine
which they continued to drink with the main course,
chicken with a minty yogurt dressing.

While they ate Reid talked about plays and art shows he had been to recently. It was the kind of conversation made by strangers at formal lunch parties and although his comments were interesting, Fran thought his choice of subjects irrelevant to this particular situation.

When the butler had withdrawn, leaving them to help themselves to a fruit salad with fromage frais, or to a selection of more substantial cheeses, she said, 'Why do you want a wife when you could go on having girl-friends and change them when you get bored?'

Offering her the elegant Waterford compote, its apparent fragility emphasising the powerful but equally elegant form of the hands in which it was cradled, he looked at her with unexpected sternness.

'I have a responsibility to my line. I need sons to carry on the traditions established by my predecessors.'

She found his solemnity irritating. 'Are you expecting me to provide proof of my fertility?'

Before she could add that, if he was, he could forget it, Reid said, 'No, I'm prepared to chance that.'

'Big deal!' Fran said sarcastically.

She had the feeling that Reid wouldn't hesitate to divorce her if she failed to live up to his expectations in some way.

But although he struck her as a monster of cold-hearted self-centredness, she couldn't deny that he was extraordinarily attractive. Every movement he had made since they sat down had heightened her awareness of the lean and muscular physique inside the well-cut suit and the long legs under the table. His hair was dry now but still had the sheen of health. There was nothing about him suggestive of stress or tension. He seemed entirely relaxed. Yet why did he need to arrange a businesslike marriage instead of falling in love the way people usually did?

Wondering, suddenly, if he might be in the same situation as herself, heartbroken, although it didn't seem likely, she said, 'When did you dream up this scheme?'

'It's an idea I've had for some time...probably since my contemporaries started divorcing. I have about a dozen god-children, most of whom now have step-parents, some official, some not. I don't want that for my children.'

'Did your parents stay married?'

It seemed to her that his face underwent a change. His lips didn't tighten. His eyebrows didn't draw together. But there was a subtle hardening and chilling, reminding her of the impression of formidable coldness she had received yesterday morning when they sat on opposite sides of his imposing desk.

Now they were at a table designed for a more intimate and relaxed conversation. But she sensed a change in the atmosphere and knew she had trespassed in an area of his life where she was an unwelcome intruder.

'They separated. They were never divorced,' he answered.

Fran wanted to ask how old he had been when the separation happened, but something made her hold her tongue.

Later, going back to the flat in the taxi he had laid on for her, she regretted restraining her curiosity.

When—if—two people were going to marry, there shouldn't be any 'No go' areas between them...or at least none of that nature. His past girlfriends were not her business, but his family life certainly was. She shouldn't have allowed herself to be put off. From now on she wouldn't be, she told herself firmly.

Later that afternoon, her sister rang up.

'How's it going?' Shelley knew about clearing the apartment but not about the interview with Reid.

'I've more or less finished. How are things with you?'

'Fine, but I've just been talking to Mum and she

sounds at the end of her tether. You don't think she might crack up…have a real nervous breakdown, do you?'

'She wouldn't dare,' Fran replied. 'Imagine Gran's re-action to anyone in her family going to pieces. She'd consider it letting the side down.'

But despite her cheerful response, intended to soothe Shelley's anxiety, Fran wasn't as sanguine as she sounded. Her mother's state of mind had been worrying her for some time.

'Gran's made of sterner stuff than Mum,' said her sister. 'You're like her and so am I, up to a point. But Mum's nothing like her. She takes after Grandad's sister, the one who was jilted and never really recovered.'

'Maybe…a bit. But Great-Aunt Rose wasn't strong and Mum is. There's nothing wrong with her physical health. She'll be all right, Shelley. Just give her time to get over the shock of it all.'

'I hope you're right.' Her sister didn't sound con-vinced.

'I live with her. I ought to know. In some strange way it may be harder for a woman to come to terms with the end of an unhappy marriage than to lose a husband she loved. Mum can't look back and say to herself, "Well, I can't complain because we had thirty great years which is more than lots of people do." Her marriage was one of the duds.'

'You could be right. Even though everyone else feels it was all Dad's fault they didn't get on, I think she blames herself…and I guess if she had been different, he would have been. Still, that's all in the past. What worries me is her future. She's never going to marry again, that's for sure, and she isn't equipped to stand on her own feet. Somehow, between us, we're going to have to look after her…but how?'

This was ground they had already been over several times and Fran didn't want to rehash it until she had made up her mind whether the solution offered by Reid was feasible.

By the following morning she had come to a decision. She rang Reid and told him.

'Good,' he said calmly. 'We'd better have dinner together. I'll pick you up at seven.'

It seemed a prosaic response, but then this was a practical down-to-earth union they were setting up.

Not knowing where he would take her, but assuming it would be somewhere fairly sophisticated, she wore a white silk-satin shirt and a narrow black wrap-over skirt. She cinched her waist with a wide belt and fixed large rhinestone stars in her ears.

Reid called for her in a taxi, wearing a Savile Row suit and conventional shirt with an unexpectedly flamboyant tie in wonderful Gauguinesque colours.

When she complimented him on it, he said, 'Even bankers have to break out sometimes.'

The restaurant he had chosen for the occasion was on the south bank of the Thames but high above the river with a panoramic view of the buildings on the far bank through walls made of sheets of glass. The décor was modern and minimalist, very different from the period elegance of his house in Kensington, although of course she hadn't seen his own part of it.

'You've been here before, I expect?' he said, as they sat down in leather tub chairs.

'No, as it happens I haven't.' She hoped the chef wasn't a minimalist. She had a heartier appetite than many of the people who patronised London's smart restaurants and tension always made her hungrier.

They had come directly to the restaurant without stopping off in the bar.

'Something to drink before dinner, sir?' the wine waiter enquired.

'Do you like champagne?' Reid asked her.

Fran nodded. She didn't like the cheap champagne sometimes served at weddings but she guessed that whatever he ordered would be the best.

'Let's make our decisions now, shall we?'

Reid was referring to the menu, but his choice of words reminded her of the momentous decision they were, if not exactly celebrating, at least ratifying. In theory she could back out right up to the moment of official commitment. But she knew she wasn't going to do that. The die was already cast, her future as his wife settled.

The champagne came, a bottle of vintage Dom Pérignon.

'Someone called this "psychological magic",' said Reid, raising his glass to her.

'We could do with some,' she said dryly.

'Why do you say that?'

'We don't have the usual kind of magic.' She nodded her head in the direction of a couple at another table gazing at each other as if the rest of the world had ceased to exist.

'We can easily conjure some up.' He reached for her free hand and lifted it to his lips, brushing them against the back of it and then turning it over and pressing his mouth to her palm.

Fran felt like snatching it back but managed to control the impulse and remove it from him with a semblance of graciousness. 'I don't think we should pretend anything we don't feel.' After a slight pause, she added, 'At the same time I'd rather no one else knew that it's a…a marriage of convenience. I know it would disturb my family if they realised it wasn't a love match.'

'In that case we're going to have to put on a show of amorous feelings in front of them,' said Reid, his expression sardonic.

'Yes…up to a point,' she acknowledged. 'When will you make it public?'

'Unfortunately I'm committed to going overseas, leaving tomorrow. I shan't be back for ten days. When I am, we can meet each other's families before putting a notice in *The Times* to let all our friends know.'

He gave her an unexpectedly charming smile. 'I would rather not go away just now, but a lot of arrangements are in place and it would cause great inconvenience if I were to cancel the trip. I'm sorry about it.'

'That's all right. It will give me more time to get used to the idea.'

'Or to change your mind.'

'If I wasn't certain, I wouldn't be here,' she said firmly. 'Once I make up my mind, that's it. I'm not a ditherer.'

'Neither am I.'

She had half expected that he might produce an heirloom ring to seal their bond. But perhaps that rite came after he had presented her to his grandmother and possibly some of the aunts he had mentioned.

'Do you have brothers and sisters?' she asked. Siblings hadn't been mentioned in the file on him, although the report on her had referred to her sister and brother-in-law.

'Unfortunately not,' he said. 'Tell me about your sister. Do you get on well with her?'

It wasn't late when he took her back to the flat. Towards the end of dinner she had begun to wonder if he would expect to make love to her. She wasn't ready for that. In the taxi, she braced herself for the awkwardness of refusing what he might now consider an entitlement.

But her apprehension proved unnecessary. He asked the driver to drop them off at the entrance to the gardens surrounding the flats, but told him to wait there. Then Reid walked her to her door, unlocked it for her and switched on the hall light.

'Goodnight, Francesca.'

He kissed the corner of her mouth. For a fleeting moment she felt the hardness of his chin and the masculine texture of his cheek against her smoother skin.

Then he straightened. 'Don't forget to put the chain on.'

The day after her return home, when she was still debating how to broach the subject of her impending marriage, two things happened, both unexpected.

First, a large florist's box arrived. Her mother was there when she opened it. 'What gorgeous flowers. Who are they from, Fran?'

There was only one person they could be from. Fran read the card enclosed with them. In a clear and distinctive hand which it didn't take a graphologist to recognise as the writing of a strong, perhaps overbearing personality, Reid had written, no doubt in the expectation that the card would be seen by others, *I would rather be talking to you.*

'They're from someone I met in London…someone rather special. I think I'll be seeing him again.'

'What's his name? Where did you meet him?'

'His name is Reid Kennard.' Fran knew the surname wouldn't ring any bells with Mrs Turner, to whom the *Financial Times* and even the business pages of the popular newspapers were of as little interest as documents written in Sanskrit. 'We met at a party some time ago.' A small lie seemed forgivable in the circumstances. 'He's had to go overseas on business. I'm not sure when I'll be seeing him again.'

'Reid…that's an unusual name. What does he do?'

'Something in the City.' Forestalling her mother's next question, Fran said, 'He's tall and dark with grey eyes.'

'He must be very taken with you to spend so much money on flowers.'

Fran made no comment on that. She said, 'Would you do them for me? You're better at it than I am.'

'I'd love to. But they need a long drink of water before going into a vase.' Mrs Turner took them away.

Soon after this Mr Preston, their lawyer, rang up and arranged to call on them that afternoon.

'He says he has some good news for us,' Fran told her mother.

'That'll make a change.' Mrs Turner's mouth quivered. 'It's been such a dreadful year. I don't know how I'd have got through it without you, love.'

'That's what families are for…to stand by each other when the going gets rough.' Fran put an arm round her shoulders and kissed her mother's cheek.

Inwardly she shared some of her grandmother's impatience with what Gran called 'Daphne's lack of spunk', but she tried never to show it. Some people were natural survivors and some weren't. Her mother wasn't. She needed someone to lean on.

Mr Preston didn't keep them in suspense. As soon as he'd shaken hands, he said, 'I'm sure you'll be relieved to hear that certain developments since I was last in touch have put a more cheerful complexion on your situation, Mrs Turner. I don't think it's going to be necessary for you to sell this house until such time as you yourself wish to move.'

'What's happened to change things, Mr Preston?' Fran asked.

'To put it in a nutshell, Miss Turner, an offer has been made for the assets of your father's company…a very generous offer. I must make it clear that before your mother and you receive any benefit from it, the creditors have to be paid. In official order, they are the Inland Revenue, then the secured creditors, which means your father's bankers, and then the unsecured creditors. But, at the end of the day, there should be sufficient left to cover your foreseeable overheads.'

Mrs Turner burst into tears. Relief made Fran feel a bit weepy herself, but she controlled her emotions.

Before she asked Mr Preston to explain the situation in more detail, she took her mother upstairs to lie down and recover.

That evening Reid rang up. He was in New York where it was still afternoon.

'I didn't expect you to act so fast,' said Fran, after confirming that the solicitor had been to see them.

'I always act fast whenever possible. Is your mother feeling better?'

'She can't quite believe the threat of eviction is no longer hanging over us. It'll take her a few days to get used to it.'

After he had rung off, she realised she had forgotten to thank him for the flowers.

Explaining the good news to Shelley and John was more difficult. They couldn't understand how, when George Turner had been unable to raise the investment capital his business needed, someone should make a good offer *after* the business had failed.

Fran managed to blind them with science by tossing out phrases picked up from Mr Preston. But afterwards she wondered if they would put two and two together when she became engaged to a leading figure in the banking world.

CHAPTER THREE

A WEEK later Fran returned from walking the dogs to find a sleek black Porsche 911, a car she had always longed to drive, parked near the front door.

She paused to admire the classic lines of what a man she had dated, although not for long, had told her had been one of the world's most desirable vehicles since before she was born and was still an object of desire to people who knew about cars and could afford the best.

Then she walked round the side of the house to the tradesmen's entrance. In the quarry-tiled lobby the dogs had their water bowls below the hooks for their leads.

Leaving them slurping, she went into the kitchen.

'Who's the visitor, Janie?'

Janie had come to the Turners as a fifteen-year-old nursery maid when Fran was a baby. She had grown up in an orphanage, with the added disadvantage of a stammer.

She had a flair for cooking and now produced all the meals as well as supervising the three part-time helpers who did the housework and ironing.

'Gentleman to see your mum.'

Fran knew Janie wouldn't have asked his name because, except in the family, she was self-conscious about her indistinct diction.

'I took in a tea tray twenty minutes ago. Shall I make a small pot for you?'

'No, thanks, I'll have a cold drink.' Fran went to the fridge for a bottle of spring water. Filling a tall glass, she said, 'Perhaps he's after the house...heard rumours it may be for sale.'

42 THE BARTERED BRIDE

'If you ask me,' said Janie, 'we'd be better off some-where smaller. It would upset your mum at first, but she could make another garden. When you leave home, this'll be far too big for just her and me.'

Fran nodded. She wondered, not for the first time, if Janie was really resigned to a lifetime of living in some-one else's house, never having a place of her own, or a husband and children. It seemed terribly unfair when she would make a much better wife than many women who didn't have her impediment.

'I'll go and find out why he's here,' she said.

Crossing the wood-panelled hall, she was surprised to hear her mother talking in an animated way most unlike her usual manner with strangers. Whoever the visitor was, he must have a gift for bringing quiet, reserved people like Mrs Turner out of their shells.

Fran opened the door and joined them.

'Oh, you're back.' Her mother jumped up, looking pleased to the point of excitement. Not since the birth of her grandchild had she looked so radiant with delight.

Rushing across the room, she embraced Fran and kissed her. 'What a dark horse you are! Yes, I know you did give me a hint...but you made it sound as if it was just the beginning. I wasn't expecting to be asked for my consent to your marriage. Not that you need it, of course, but it's very nice to be asked.'

She turned round and beamed at Reid who had been sitting in the armchair with its back to the door, but was now on his feet, watching Fran's reaction to her mother's announcement.

The moments of silence which followed were ended by Mrs Turner saying, 'Well...you two must have a lot to talk about and I need to do some watering. You will be staying the night with us, Reid?'

'Unfortunately I can't. This is a flying visit.'

'Oh, what a pity. I thought... Still, if you can't, you can't.' She moved towards the door, to be overtaken by

Reid who held it open for her. 'Thank you.' She disappeared.

He closed the door and returned to where Fran was standing. Placing his hands on her shoulders, he looked thoughtfully down at her. 'What was the hint you gave your mother?'

She hadn't forgotten how disturbing he was at close quarters, but remembering it wasn't the same as experiencing it. The weight of his hands on her shoulders, being so near to his tall, lithe body, being subjected to a searching scrutiny all combined to make her breath catch in her throat. She felt her composure desert her. Why did he have this effect? Other men never had, not even Julian.

'I told her I'd met someone interesting...someone I might be seeing more of. Thank you for all the flowers and cards.'

'My pleasure...but isn't a verbal thank-you rather formal from a wife-to-be to her future husband? Wouldn't a kiss be more appropriate?'

She was wearing an old pair of deck shoes. Rising on her toes, with her palms on his chest for balance, she lifted her lips to his cheek.

'Still too formal,' said Reid. An arm went round her, drawing her firmly against him in a light but close chest-to-breast, thigh-to-thigh contact. His other hand circled her neck, the pad of his thumb tilting the base of her chin.

Just being in his arms was enough to make her heart pound. There could be no glancing away from his searching gaze. The only way *not* to meet his eyes was to close her own, and she didn't want to do that. It might convey the wrong message.

'Why are you nervous?' he asked. 'I'm not going to bite you. Not yet. That's for later, when we know each other much better...and even then they'll be very gentle bites. You'll like them...and so shall I.'

He had lowered his voice to a deeper, more intimate tone and the look in his eyes was so different from the coldness of his first appraisal the day she had gone to the bank that she found it hard to believe this was the same man.

He was making love to her, she realised. Using his voice to caress her and make her respond. He was obviously very experienced. How would he react when he found out that she wasn't? That kissing was as far as she had gone, because everything else she had been willing to wait for until she could share it with Julian.

Julian. Somehow her memory of him wasn't as sharp as it had been. Once every detail of his face had been as clear in her mind's eye as the features of the man looking down at her. But that was beginning to change. She still felt pain when she thought of him. But not as intensely, and not while Reid was holding her and sending little shivers through her.

'I didn't think you'd be back till the weekend,' she murmured, postponing the moment when he would bend his head.

'The original plan was to spend it with an American banker and his family. When I explained the circumstances they let me take a rain check.'

'What did you tell them?'

'That'd I'd just become engaged and wanted to get back to you.'

'But now you say you can't even stay the night.'

'My grandmother's expecting me to meet her at the airport. She's been staying in the south of France with my senior aunt. They're both coming over to meet you. Why don't you come down by train some time tomorrow? Then the following day I'll bring you back in the car. We might call on your sister *en route*...get all the introductions over and done with.'

'How did your grandmother take it? Wasn't she very surprised?'

'She was delighted. She's been urging me to marry for years.'

Before Fran could ask another question, he swooped like a hawk and kissed her, not, this time, on the corner of her mouth but full on the lips.

Compared with some of the slobbery, tongue-thrusting goodnight kisses she had experienced at parties and on several first-and-last dates, Reid's kiss was restrained and gentle. Yet it had more effect than any of the hungry, heavy-breathing kisses.

There had been a few times when men had kissed her nicely, but never as nicely as this. It was actually a succession of mini-kisses, each one a soft momentary pressure in a fractionally different place, sometimes more on her upper lip and sometimes more on her lower. The effect was startlingly enjoyable.

By the time he stopped, instinct was urging her to slide her arms round his neck. As she opened her eyes, Fran saw that he was smiling.

For a few seconds she thought he was going to kiss her again, this time with less restraint. Instead he released her and stepped back, causing a twinge of disappointment and making her wonder if he hadn't found the experience as pleasant as she had.

'You've been out with the dogs, I hear. What sort of dogs?'

'A Labrador and a whippet. They were my sister's until she got married. She and John were living in a minuscule cottage, both working flat out to raise money to set up the nursery, so the dogs were an encumbrance. It was better for them to stay here. It's where they've always lived. When I go, Janie will walk them. She likes them and they like her.'

'Janie?'

'Our "treasure"'—wiggling her forefingers. 'The person who opened the door to you.'

'Does she live in?'

'Yes, she's been with us for years.'

'How will your mother cope with life on her own when you leave home?'

'It won't bother her. She's a naturally solitary person. It was having to leave the garden that was wrecking her. Her plants are her closest companions. She talks to them.'

'My other grandmother does that. It sounds as if she and your mother have a lot in common,' said Reid. He looked at his watch. 'I must go if I'm going to be at the airport on time.'

'It was a long way to come for such a short stay...especially when you must be tired from your trip.'

But he didn't look jet-lagged, she thought. He had the air of someone who has just come back from a holiday on a high of energy and vitality.

Fran went with him to the car where, having unlocked it, he took off the coat of his suit and tossed it in the back. Then he took off his tie, a more conservative choice than the one he had worn when they dined together.

'I thought I'd better look respectable when I came to ask for your hand,' he said, rolling the tie round his fingers, his mouth straight but his eyes amused.

'How ought I to dress to make a good impression on your family?' Fran asked.

He looked at the sweatshirt, jeans and deck shoes she had put on to walk the dogs.

'From what I've seen so far, you have an impeccable dress sense. Wear whatever seems appropriate.'

He put the tie in the car and unbuttoned the neckband of what, from the way it fitted the extra-broad span of his shoulders, had to be a made-to-measure shirt. With the collar open, exposing the base of his throat, he looked younger and less formidable.

'By the way, I hope you don't want an elaborate wedding. They take too long to organise. Also it seems to be one of Murphy's laws that the more elaborate the wedding, the less chance there is of the couple making a go of it. I'm thinking of most of the weddings I've been to over the last ten years...and I've been to a lot.'

'So have I and you're right,' she agreed. 'There's also the point that a white dress and yards of veil look incredibly bogus when everyone knows the bride and groom have been sleeping together, if not living together, for so long that the honeymoon will just be another holiday for them.'

He lifted an eyebrow. 'But would you have wanted to live in the days when the dress and the veil weren't merely nods to tradition and the honeymoon, at least for the bride, was a voyage into unknown territory?'

For a moment she considered putting her cards on the table, saying bluntly, 'That's what it will be for me. I've never slept with anyone. I'll be a virgin bride.'

Some instinct she couldn't analyse restrained her. 'I wouldn't have minded. I'm not sure that, all in all, today's way is so much better. There are just as many unhappy people as there ever were. But now they're unhappy singles instead of being miserable in pairs. My parents didn't get on, but Shelley and I didn't know that till later. I'm sure we felt much more secure than if Mum had been a single parent. I don't think she could have coped.'

Reid undid another button, giving a glimpse of a chest that, even more than his face, was still brown from time in the sun.

'They say that before a man marries he should take a close look at his prospective mother-in-law, because that's what her daughter will be like in twenty or thirty years' time. If you're going to turn out like yours, that will be fine with me. She seems a very nice woman, even if she and your father weren't an ideally matched couple.'

'What makes you think you and I are?'

'I trust my judgment. When you've decided what train to catch, leave a message on my answering machine. I'll come and meet you. Goodbye, Francesca.' He blew her a kiss before sliding his long frame into the driving seat.

She watched the car glide down the drive. Before turning out of the gate, he put his arm out of the window and gave her a final wave.

Fran raised a hand, half regretting that she hadn't turned away as soon as he started the engine. She had the feeling she ought to be playing it cooler instead of surrendering all control of the situation to him.

She went to see if her mother needed help with the watering. It had been a dry winter and already there was a hosepipe ban in place which Mrs Turner observed with more conscientiousness than some of her neighbours, even though carrying cans made her back ache.

'Has he gone already?' she asked, as her daughter joined her, a full can in either hand.

'Yes. What do you think of him?'

'He's got lovely manners. Gran will be thrilled. He's the sort of young man she hoped you'd marry. But how long have you known him, love? It all seems to have happened very quickly.'

'I wanted to keep it quiet until I was sure,' said Fran, knowing the truth would horrify her mother and start her worrying again. 'Reid felt the same way. I haven't met his family yet. I'm going to meet some of them tomorrow. I'm not sure they'll think as highly of me as you do of him.'

'I don't know why they shouldn't,' said Mrs Turner, a touch indignantly. 'Most people would count themselves lucky if their son took home a girl half as nice as you.'

'You're prejudiced, Mum,' Fran said, smiling.

'No, I'm not. You *are* a nice girl...a lovely girl. Neither you nor Shelley gave me or your Dad a moment's worry...not like some people's daugh-

ters…staying out till all hours…sleeping around…
smoking and drinking and worse. You've never done
any of that.'

Only because I was waiting for Julian, thought Fran.
If I hadn't been in love with him, I might have tried
everything on offer.

To steer away from this topic, she said, 'We're not
going to have a big wedding so you don't need to worry
about organising the kind of show Dad insisted Shelley
must have. She didn't want all that fuss. It was his idea.'

Like many self-made men, her father had seized every
opportunity to show off. Her sister had walked up the
aisle followed by six small bridesmaids and three maids
of honour, the bill for her dress and theirs running to
thousands of pounds. Not to mention the cost of the
lavish floral arrangements and a sit-down wedding
breakfast for three hundred people.

Fran had never wanted that sort of show but, day-
dreaming about her marriage to Julian, she had designed
a succession of white bridal dresses. In her mind's eye,
she had always arrived at the church veiled in a cloud
of diaphanous tulle.

'But you will have a church wedding, won't you?'
Mrs Turner asked.

'I don't know yet. Possibly not. We haven't discussed
the details.'

Her mother looked at Fran's left hand. 'When are you
choosing the ring?'

'I don't know that either. Reid may have a family ring
he wants me to wear.'

Fran gave a great deal of thought to how best to present
herself to Reid's grandmother who, although she might
or might not be a major influence on him personally,
was clearly the matriarch of the family and therefore
someone whose approval would smooth Fran's path.

She remembered the girls at her boarding-school,

who, when they arrived, had been in one of three categories: the daughters of Old Money families, the daughters of Newly Rich parents, and the girls whose backgrounds were unimportant because they had brilliant brains.

Later on there had been other divisions: girls who excelled at games, girls who were natural leaders, unpopular girls and amusing girls who, more often than not, were also girls with a weight problem.

By the time they left school, the divisions were less apparent. They had all been changed by mixing with each other and by the school's ethos. It aimed to produce young women who would have an influence on society, either in the world at large or—as they were regularly reminded—in the equally important sphere of family life.

Fran had been a leading member of the school's dramatic society but had never had showbiz ambitions. She knew she could easily present herself as the Sloane Ranger type of girl most conventional upper crust women would want their grandsons to marry. She had clothes in her wardrobe which fitted that image. But she wasn't really a Sloane so why put on an act? Why not just be herself and chance the old bird's disapproval?

Which still left her in a quandary because she had often felt that, personality-wise, she was like an iceberg. The part of her that showed was the Fran Turner other people wanted her to be. But there was a mass of potential under the surface. She had always sensed there was more to her than met the eye, but had been drifting along, obsessed by Julian and an idyllic future which, as matters had turned out, was never going to materialise.

Now she felt she was waiting for some titanic event which would reveal what she was really made of. Maybe this process had already begun. Maybe the uncharacteristic flare of anger which had made her storm out of Reid's office had been the beginning of it.

In the end she went to London wearing the two things she would snatch from her wardrobe if the house was on fire. One was a light silk raincoat, the colour of a black grape, bought in New York where smart women wore similar coats to go to the theatre and restaurants.

Under this she wore a delicious extravagance found a few weeks before her father's business crashed. It was French, from a shop where the prices were such that the door was kept locked and customers had to press a bell for admittance.

She saw Reid waiting for her before he spotted her. His height and the way he carried himself made him stand out even in the crowded concourse of a main-line railway station. As it happened the way he was dressed was less conformist than anything she had seen him in so far. He was wearing a soft suede windcheater, the colour of butterscotch, with grey trousers and a grey silk shirt, open at the neck. He didn't look like a banker, even an off-duty banker. She wasn't sure what he looked like...except that the sight of him gave her an undeniable buzz.

But it wasn't anything like the feeling she had had when Julian came home. That had been a more soulful, less physical reaction.

'Hello.' He kissed her cheek and took charge of her overnight case. 'I don't use the car in London. We'll get a taxi.'

As they joined the line-up for cabs, Reid said, 'Your hair looks magnificent.'

'Thank you.'

For each of their previous meetings it had been under restraint, held with pins or a clip or, yesterday, with a ruffle of ribbon on an elastic core.

Today she'd decided to go for the big-hair look, brushing it into a cloud of resplendent redness which had made her mother say doubtfully, 'Oh, Franny, love, do you think…?' And then, typically, quash her doubts with, 'Well, I expect you know best.'

'Is that colour natural?' he asked, after they had secured a cab.

'Yes, but my eyelashes aren't. That's one thing your investigator missed out. I have them professionally darkened. My eyebrows as well. But otherwise I'm as nature intended.' She bared her teeth in a broad smile. 'No caps, no implants…what you see is what you get.'

'And very nice too. I like this.' He touched the earring nearest to him, a flamboyant silver hoop set with tiny chunks of unpolished turquoise. 'Which reminds me…'

He felt in his pocket and produced a small leather box. 'I did some impulse shopping in New York. It may not fit your engagement finger or you may prefer something more classic. If so, you can wear it as a dress ring. Someone else at the bank who's recently got engaged took his girlfriend to a goldsmith who designed her wedding and engagement rings as a complementary pair.'

Opening the box, he showed Fran a ring for which if, a few months ago, it had caught her eye in a Bond Street jeweller's window, she would have willingly gone into overdraft.

Unlike her earrings, which were inexpensive costume pieces, this was a serious jewel, a combination of aquamarine, emerald and sapphire set in a swirl of gold which had to have been inspired by the designer leaning on the rail of a yacht, looking down through the sunlit surface into the depths of the sea.

'I thought it went with your eyes…and your hair,' said Reid. 'Try it on. See if it fits.'

She was not sure what made her say, 'I think you should put it on for me.' And then add, 'That's the usual form, isn't it?'

'I wouldn't know. I've never been engaged before.' His eyebrow went up. 'Have you?'

'Uh-uh.' She shook her head, fanning the fingers of her left hand and holding them towards him.

He took the ring from its velvet bed. The lid of the case was lined with matching satin gold-stamped with the name of a famous Fifth Avenue jeweller. He slid the ring over her knuckle and settled it in place, his fingertips making contact with the sensitive webs of skin between her fingers and sending a flash of sensation shooting up her arm.

'It might have been made for me,' she said, turning her hand this way and that to admire the effect. 'It's a wonderful ring. Thank you, Reid.'

And then, swept by an impulse which had a lot more to do with that erotic reaction than with complying with 'form', she put her hand up to his head, took a gentle hold of his ear and, drawing his face down to hers, gave him a soft-lipped kiss, full on the mouth.

What happened next was as disconcerting as her impulse. Outwardly, nothing happened. Her fingers released his ear and their heads drew apart. But neither of them looked away and Fran knew, from the heat in Reid's eyes that, in a culture that permitted it, he would have grabbed her and made for the nearest place where they would be undisturbed while he gave rein to his instincts.

But as they were civilised people in a taxi in the heart of London, he was forced to restrain his urges and to say, 'I'm glad you like it,' while dealing, as best he could, with a reaction which she hadn't intended to arouse and could only deal with by pretending a sudden interest in the passing scene.

As she averted her face, showing him the lovely line from her cheekbone to her jaw, Reid felt like hauling her into his arms and returning the kiss with interest. Had it been dark he would have done so.

The driver had closed the glass partition when they got in. With a fare on their own he might chat, glance in the rear-view mirror or, at traffic lights, even turn round to look at the person behind him.

With a couple on the back seat, one a sensational girl, he would keep his eyes on the road. But at this time of day pedestrians could catch a glimpse of a couple embracing and Reid preferred to do his necking in private.

His grandmother and his aunt both kept fairly early hours. Tonight, after they had retired, there would be plenty of time to resume what Francesca had started. He expected to spend the night in her bedroom. His grandmother would certainly disapprove and even his more broad-minded aunt might not entirely condone it. But he doubted if sex had ever been among their pleasures, even when they were younger. They were both the sort of women who, during their fertile years, had lain back and thought about their herbaceous borders.

Francesca's passionate mouth and, sometimes, her body language made it obvious she wouldn't be like that...once she got over her understandable reservations about the pragmatic nature of their relationship.

At the moment, although she was doing a good job of not showing it, he was aware of the tension she felt about meeting his family. That was understandable. His grandmother would undoubtedly classify George Turner as 'an absolute bounder', and with justification.

But Reid knew that his grandmother's choice of a suitable bride for him would bore him out of his mind. He had problems enough without adding an incompatible wife to the existing difficulties of his life.

Sneaking a covert glance at him, Fran was dismayed to see that while he was looking at the back of the driver's head rather than at her, his face suggested that, although he had been turned on a few minutes ago, his mood at this moment was one of extreme displeasure.

The set of his mouth was severe, not to say grim. It was hard to believe her kiss was the cause of that glowering expression. But clearly something was annoying him.

Then the forbidding look lightened and he turned his head and said pleasantly, 'I expect you're feeling a bit nervous. Meeting one's future in-laws is always like walking through a minefield. But what any of them think isn't really important. The only person we have to get along with is each other.'

It was meant to be reassuring and, up to a point, it was. But she couldn't help wondering if the subtext was that he knew his relations wouldn't like her but didn't care because he had never cared for anyone else's opinion...and when they were married would disregard hers as well.

The knowledge that they were virtually strangers with nothing in common beyond a strong physical attraction made her wonder if the beautiful ring she was wearing was a token she would come to wish she had never accepted.

Lady Kennard and her daughter, Mrs Onslow, were not unlike Gran and Mum in that one was bossy and the other compliant. Fran saw that in the first five minutes of their acquaintance.

She also saw that there the resemblance ended. Both these women were stuck in a time warp, their outlook and values those of an era that had passed and most people had forgotten, if they ever knew it existed.

'Are you an actress?' asked Lady Kennard, taking in Fran's appearance and clearly deciding that only someone in the theatre would wear her hair like that and dress in such extraordinary garments.

'No, I don't have a career. I live at home with my mother...like the girls in Jane Austen's novels,' Fran said demurely.

'But with rather more freedom than they enjoyed,' was Reid's dry comment.

As she glanced at him, his eyes swept over her outfit and she wondered what he thought of it.

A housekeeper had taken her up to a comfortable bedroom where she had hung up her coat and unpacked her case. Then she had found her way to the drawing room where Reid had introduced her to these two women, both wearing pearls and clothes of excellent quality but totally lacking in style.

'How unusual,' said Lady Kennard. 'Most of the girls one knows have filled in the time between leaving school and marriage with some occupation...working at Sotheby's, or cooking directors' lunches. My daughters' daughters have all worked for a few years.'

'Most people do,' Fran agreed. 'But I didn't need to or want to. I found other things to do. Did you have a career, Lady Kennard?'

Looking surprised at having a question lobbed back at her, Reid's grandmother said, 'No, I didn't. But when I was young few girls did. Tell me...'

Her inquisition continued until Reid, looking bored, cut it short by saying, 'Before it's time for drinks, I want to give Francesca a quick tour of my part of the house.'

She was glad to escape. She wasn't sure what Mrs Onslow thought of her, but it didn't take much intuition to divine Lady Kennard's opinion. They were never going to be buddies.

Outside the room, Reid took her by the hand and swept her up the staircase to a floor where the ceilings weren't as high or the architectural details as grand as those on the first floor.

He said, 'I'm sorry about the third degree. My grandmother hasn't learnt to take people as she finds them. She's not at ease with glamour.'

'Glamour?' Fran queried. It was a word she associated with long-dead film stars, platinum blondes in bias-cut, backless satin evening dresses, brunettes with Cupid'sbow lips looking seductively over white fox-furred shoulders.

They had reached the next highest landing which was still not the top of the house. There was another above it and above that a large glazed cupola shedding light right down to the hall.

'Glamour,' Reid repeated. 'You look a knock-out and you know it.'

'I don't think your grandmother thinks so.'

'Possibly not, but I do.' His eyes had narrowed. They glittered with the same light she had seen in the taxi after kissing him. 'Take off the jacket.'

Her outfit consisted of three parts; a loose hip-length coat of diaphanous printed silk georgette bound at the edges with velvet ribbon, a silk-lined chemise with ribbon shoulder straps, and a skirt made of several layers, with rolled hems that rose and fell to show the layer beneath and to float around her when she moved.

But it wasn't her clothes Reid was studying as she slipped off the jacket but the contours revealed or suggested by the sheer, fluid fabric. 'I'll show you my book room later. Right now...'

He propelled her through a door, closed it and took her in his arms.

It was like being caught by a whirlwind, or some other force of nature which couldn't be escaped or resisted so the only thing to do was nothing. She could feel her heart starting to pound and excitement tinged with panic flooding her body. He was holding the small of her back, his fingers splayed to support her as he swayed her backwards, his mouth demanding a response.

She knew this was a reprisal for the kiss in the taxi which perhaps he had seen as a come-on, although that was not her intention.

Her eyes closed, every nerve in her body quivering, Fran surrendered to a kiss far beyond her experience although not beyond her imagination. This was how she had dreamed of being kissed...by Julian.

But the strong arm now locked round her waist, the hand stroking her back, the aftershave, the slightly abrasive male chin she could feel nudging hers, the lips commanding her lips, none of these were Julian's.

Simultaneously, as her body was telling her, Yes! This is what you were made for, the sharp voice of conscience was saying, No! This is wrong. You aren't in love with this man. You shouldn't be doing this with him.

When at last Reid let her go, she was still torn between desire and doubt.

Reid was smiling, his colour high, the message in his eyes unmistakable. He wanted her and knew that she wanted him.

She was still holding the gauzy coat. He took it from her and tossed it onto a chair. Then, as she was catching her breath, trying to recover herself, he stepped behind her and she felt his fingers brushing the skin between her shoulder blades.

But, her head in a whirl of confusion, she didn't immediately grasp what he was doing: unfastening the three silk-looped buttons at the back of the chemise. It was only when he moved the velvet straps over the ends of her shoulders that she realised he was undressing her.

At the same time she realised the room they were in was a bedroom...his bedroom.

Underneath the chemise she was wearing a strapless bra. Before he could undo that, she clutched the chemise to her front and whirled round to face him.

'No...please...not now...not yet...'

'There's plenty of time before we need reappear.' He closed the gap, his hands caressing her shoulders. 'Your skin feels as smooth as marble, but softer...warmer.' His voice was husky, persuasive.

Fran jerked away, out of reach. She could see she would have to speak plainly. 'I don't want to make love yet. I'd rather wait till we're married.'

CHAPTER FOUR

SHE thought he would scowl and say something coldly sarcastic.

But although he stopped smiling, his tone was mild as he said, 'Sweetheart, a moment ago, you were—'

'You surprised me. I hadn't realised this was your bedroom. I didn't mean to...lead you on.'

He lifted an eyebrow. 'Francesca—' the soft way he said her name made her insides turn over—'you turn me on every time you look at me. I want you and you want me. Let's do something about it? There's a tedious evening ahead of us. My grandmother doesn't go to bed that early. She may not turn in till eleven or later.'

'I'm sure she wouldn't like it if she thought we were making love under her roof.'

'She's going to assume that anyway. As long as we don't advertise it, I don't think she'll give a fig. She's accepted that nice girls do. Possibly not her own daughters, but their daughters...yes, no question. Even if she and my aunt knew we were here instead of in the book room, it wouldn't damn you in their eyes. Stop worrying about it.'

His hands were on her shoulders, his thumbs caressing her collarbones.

'It's not only that. I don't want to go to bed with you now.'

'Why? Wrong time of the month?'

Julian, the nearest she had come to having a brother although she had never seen him in that light, would never have asked such a personal question.

Tempted to take the easy way out of this situation by

letting Reid think that was her reason, she hesitated. But she didn't want to lie to him and anyway this was an issue better confronted now. If it wasn't settled, it might crop up again between now and their wedding.

'No, it's not that. I've never had sex with people I hardly know. It's just not my style.'

He seemed more amused than annoyed. 'It's not mine either,' he said dryly. 'But we are engaged to be married and I can't see any good reason to postpone a pleasure we both want.'

He would have kissed her again but she fended him off and, although he could easily have overcome her resistance, he didn't.

'You're not on the pill. Is that it?' he suggested.

'No, I'm not. That's *one* of the reasons.'

'Then stop worrying. I'll take care of it. I agree that it might be better to postpone having babies for a while...although not for too long. My father was in his sixties when I was a teenager. I'd like to be younger than that when our sons are growing up.'

Fran took a deep breath. 'Reid, you're missing the point. I don't *want* to make love today...or tomorrow...or any time before we're married. That might seem very old-fashioned but it's the way I feel. If...if you don't have enough confidence to take that side of our relationship on trust, then you shouldn't be marrying me. I'm prepared to believe that you'll be a considerate lover.'

He was still holding her shoulders but his fingers were motionless on her bare skin. He looked at her for a long time. She couldn't tell what he was thinking. If he guessed the truth, would he see it as a pro or a con?

At last he said, 'Very well, if that's the way you want it, that's the way it will be. Turn round and I'll button you up.'

She turned round, replacing the straps where they had been before he pushed them aside.

Suddenly, when she thought he was still busy with the buttons, he put his lips to her back, a few inches down from her nape.

'But let's just get one thing straight,' he said, speaking close to her ear. 'If by "considerate lover" you mean one of those twin-bed marriages with a mistress in the background, forget it. I don't want a sexy mistress. I want a passionate wife. There's more to marriage than good sex…a lot more. But sex is a key ingredient. I hope we're agreed on that.'

'Of course.'

She refrained from adding that she didn't see how making love could ever be sublime unless both partners truly loved each other with all their hearts, which was never going to be true in their case.

They might, as time went on, develop a strong affection for each other. But love was something else, an extra dimension only a lucky few experienced. Presumably Julian felt that way about Alice, although it was hard to see why.

Fran had been baffled by what he could see in her that wasn't apparent to the rest of the world. Alice's giggle would have driven her mad. She seemed a most unlikely person for a brilliantly clever man to choose as his life's companion.

As they left the bedroom Fran slipped on the georgette jacket. Not that the chemise was particularly *décolleté* but she felt that the less bare skin she had on show the better. If her senses were still vibrating, Reid's must be too.

His book room was a delight. Every inch of the walls was covered with packed shelves or pictures. The only furniture was two comfortable sofas—both large enough for someone his size to stretch out on—an antique library table stacked with brand-new books and a print stand for looking at drawings.

Wandering around, reading the titles of his books and

studying the pictures while he lounged on the arm of a sofa, watching her, she was struck by the diversity of his interests. There were whole shelves of books on subjects ranging from history and philosophy to martial arts, jazz and photography.

That the evening wasn't as dull as Reid had forecast was entirely due to him. At dinner he dominated the conversation, often being very funny. He was an unexpectedly good mimic with an international repertoire of accents.

Fran was beginning to wonder if she was up to his weight. But maybe a clever, witty wife wasn't what he wanted. He might prefer to hold the stage on his own with his wife a member of the audience.

She wasn't sure she was comfortable with that concept. She saw an ideal marriage as an alliance between two people who, although their contributions to the match might be different, were on a more or less equal footing.

She wanted a husband she could admire and respect, but not one who made her feel the inferior partner. She knew she had many shortcomings, but most of her life she had felt good about herself and even the trauma of losing her one true love hadn't changed her innate sense of self-worth.

After dinner Mrs. Onslow said there was something she wanted to watch on TV. Reid also wanted to see it. But Lady Kennard said, 'Francesca and I will stay here and talk.'

Without being ungracious, it was difficult for Fran to get out of this tête-à-tête. Reid, had he wished, could have rescued her, but he chose not to.

When the others had gone to wherever the television lived, Lady Kennard beckoned Fran to a chair nearer to her and subjected her to another grilling.

'My grandson can be very charming, but he won't be an easy man to live with,' she remarked.

'Do you find him difficult to live with?' Fran asked.

Lady Kennard's gesture dismissed the question as irrelevant, even impertinent. 'We expected him to marry someone outstandingly gifted either in his own field or perhaps in the arts. All his previous young women have had successful careers. I'm very surprised that you haven't.'

'Perhaps he thinks my home-making skills are superior,' Fran suggested.

It was all too apparent that, without actually saying so point-blank, this stuck-up old harridan disapproved of Reid's choice.

The one question she hadn't asked, and the only really important one, was, 'Do you love my grandson?'

The evening concluded with a cup of hot chocolate for Lady Kennard, a tisane for her daughter who had lived in France since her husband's retirement, and a glass of cognac for Reid. Fran, who had asked for a glass of spring water, looked enviously at Reid's brandy. She could have done with a stiff nightcap.

They all went upstairs together, his aunt's and his grandmother's rooms being closer to the staircase than Fran's. When they had disappeared, Reid walked with her to her door.

'Did you manage to hold your own with Granny K?' he asked.

'I don't know. She made it clear she doesn't think much of me...but I'm not mad about her,' she added frankly.

'One doesn't choose one's relations,' he said dryly. 'You won't have to see much of her. Goodnight. Sleep well. There's no need to lock your door. I accept your embargo. This isn't going to be a long engagement. I can wait.'

His goodnight kiss was a chaste salute on her forehead.

*   *   *

After an early breakfast on their own, as both Mrs Onslow and her mother preferred to breakfast in bed, Reid and Fran set out to visit his other grandmother.

Once out of London, on the motorway, he was able to let the car out. Fran had expected it to be ultra-comfortable but had wondered what sort of driver he was. She had done well in an Advanced Driver's test and was happier being at the wheel than in the passenger seat.

Reid's performance on the motorway quickly reassured her that he was neither a speed freak nor a road hog. He drove fast, but never beyond the legal limit and his courtesy to other drivers was exemplary.

Mrs Heatherley lived in an old manor house near Oxford. Fran's first sight of her was of an ample behind up-ended over a flower bed near the manor's stone porch.

In an upright position, Reid's other grandmother had a friendly weather-beaten face, grey hair crammed into the crown of a panama hat and a bosom to match her comfortable hips.

'Reid, darling…lovely to see you.' As he bent down to hug her, she gave him a smacking kiss. 'And this is Francesca.' Without waiting to be introduced, she gripped Fran's upper arms and planted a slightly more restrained kiss on her cheek. 'I've been dying to meet you since Reid rang up and told me he had finally met his fate. About time too. I was beginning to think he would never find someone to take him on.'

Beaming, she shepherded them indoors where, in a cosy untidy room with several large dogs lying about and lots of flowers, she had a bottle of champagne on ice.

'So when and where is the wedding to be?' she asked, having drunk to their health and happiness.

On the drive down, Reid had revealed that, subject to Fran's agreement, he had made a tentative booking for their marriage to take place at his local register office in a fortnight's time.

Now he looked at her and raised his eyebrows. She'd had a little over an hour to consider it. He expected her to have made up her mind.

Actually she had done that almost immediately. If she were going to take this extraordinary gamble with her future, there was no point in delaying it.

When she nodded, he told Mrs Heatherley, adding, 'With only our closest relations present.'

His grandmother nodded approvingly. 'Very sensible of you, Francesca. I've always thought big fancy weddings an outrageous waste of money. My mother bullied me into having one and by the time it was over I was far too exhausted to enjoy the beginning of our honeymoon. I was a virgin, of course, as many girls were in those days, so that was an added stress. Luckily my darling Robert couldn't have been more understanding so it didn't end in tears as so many wedding nights did.'

She moved to a table and picked up a framed photograph of a man in an open-necked shirt with wind-ruffled hair. 'This is Robert when he was Reid's age. They're rather alike, don't you think?'

Reid had already told Fran that his maternal grandfather, a dedicated climber, had been killed in the Himalaya when he was in his forties. She could see some resemblance between them. They both had dark hair, large bony noses and strong chins. But Robert Heatherley's face looked more easygoing and open.

'Yes, they are,' she agreed, wondering how, if theirs had been a love match, the smiling woman beside her had survived the years of anxiety and, finally, the fatal accident.

'It's a shame they never knew each other. They would have got on so well. Now you must be hungry. Let's go and have lunch. As it's a mild day, we'll eat outside in my sun-trap. I'd better lend you a shady hat, Francesca.

With that gorgeous hair and fair skin, I expect you have to be careful not to burn.'

They said goodbye at four. As they drove away, *en route* to see Shelley and John, Fran felt much more relaxed than she had the night before. Like Lady Kennard, Mrs Heatherley had asked her a lot of questions but in a friendlier way. The rapport had been mutual. Fran felt it would be a pleasure to spend more time at the manor with someone who, like her mother, had found solace in her garden.

Reid's thoughts were running on similar lines. 'You seemed to hit it off well.'

'Who wouldn't? She's such a dear.'

Suddenly it struck Fran that one person who hadn't been mentioned during four hours' conversation was Mrs Heatherley's daughter...Reid's mother. She wondered why not but hesitated to ask. The fact that neither of them had made any reference to her suggested that something had happened to Mrs Kennard which had been even more painful than the premature death of Miranda Heatherley's husband.

They spent most of the journey listening to the first part of an audio travel book read by a well-known actor. It was restful to sit in silence, watching the passing scenery with the actor's mellifluous voice telling the story of a journey through Asia. It took Fran back to her childhood. Some of her happiest times had been listening to Gran telling true stories about her own childhood.

As they approached the village where Shelley and her family lived, Fran wondered what Reid would make of a lifestyle so remote from his own.

As people, he could hardly fail to like John and her sister, although he might not think much of their domestic arrangements, especially having two small children underfoot all the time. But the visit would be a preparation for the meeting with Gran.

Fran was uneasy about that. Gran was shrewd. To use one of her own favourite phrases, she might smell a rat. If she did, she wouldn't be discreet. She'd voice her suspicions, loud and clear. Fran had lost count of the times she had heard her grandmother say, 'If there's one thing I can't abide it's folk being underhanded.'

'Shall we leave the car at the pub and walk to your sister's place?' Reid suggested, as they entered the village.

'Good idea.' She wondered if he had suggested it as a tactful way of not turning up in a luxurious car far beyond her brother-in-law's means.

Being unable to put them up, Shelley had booked two rooms, which Fran would pay for, at The Plough, a public house that did bed and breakfast. It remained to be seen whether the accommodation would be of a standard Reid found acceptable. But it was only for one night.

The Plough had a garden at the back which ran down to a stream. The car park was at the side. Reid parked next to a tractor, whose driver must be having a beer on his way home, and a van with lengths of piping sticking out of the back door.

Taking their overnight cases from the back seat, he followed Fran into the pub which had a lounge bar on one side of the hall and a snug on the other. As they entered, the landlord's wife was coming from the rear of the premises with a tray of home-made sausage rolls.

She knew Fran by sight. 'Shan't keep you two ticks, Miss Turner. Good evening, sir.'

Seconds later she bustled back. 'I'm afraid my two best rooms had already been booked by two of my regulars when your sister rang up. I've had to put you in the attics. But I think you'll be comfortable, just for the one night.'

She led the way up the stairs, chatting over her shoulder about the more spring-like weather.

The doors of the rooms at the top of the house stood

open, showing sloping ceilings, small dormer windows and fresh-looking flowery wallpaper.

'They've both got their own basins. The bath and toilet are in here.' She opened the door of a smaller room lit by a skylight. 'I'd suggest you have the double-bedded room, sir...being so tall. It's a nice big old-fashioned bed, more roomy for someone with long legs. I'll leave you to settle in.'

Leaving his case on the landing, Reid put Fran's on one of the twin beds and went to the window to look out. 'There are chickens in the orchard across the stream. Perhaps we'll get real eggs for breakfast.'

'Probably.' Fran opened her case and began to unpack the few things it contained.

Although they had separate rooms, there was something peculiarly intimate about being the only people sleeping on this floor and sharing the bathroom. She wondered if, later, Reid would try to persuade her to share the big double bed.

He turned round and came to stand beside her. 'You're a very neat packer.'

'Is that a surprise?' she asked.

'No...but you can't always tell. Some apparently organised people prove to be anything but when you get to know them. I would find it hard to live with someone who was chronically untidy.'

'Someone obsessively orderly might be equally irritat—' She broke off as he turned her towards him and took her face between his hands.

'Just to remind you that we are engaged...' He kissed her lightly on the lips.

Then he let her go and walked out of the room, closing the door behind him.

Her knees suddenly wobbly, Fran sat down on the bed. She found herself wishing this was a pub somewhere in Wales or Scotland and they were on their honeymoon, all the formalities over, the knot tied and only the final hurdle of their wedding night still to come. In which case, of course, they would be in the room with the big double bed and he would carry on kissing her.

Thoughts of where this might lead made her close her eyes and lie back, overwhelmed by a powerful longing to rid herself of the gift she had been reserving for Julian but which he hadn't wanted.

As she lay there, imagining herself being made love to by someone she scarcely knew, there was a light tap on the door and, before she could disengage her imagination and switch back to reality, it opened and Reid walked in.

'Are you tired?' he asked.

'No...' Fran hoisted herself into a sitting position. 'I was just trying out the mattress. I like a fairly hard one.'

'I see.' His expression suggested that he recognised an improvisation when he heard one. 'I thought I'd have a quick shower. I came in to ask if you'd like to use the bathroom before I go in there.'

'No, thanks.'

'I shan't be long.' He withdrew.

It had been considerate of him to ask, she thought. But she wished he hadn't come in and found her lying down. He might guess it had something to do with his kiss and be amused.

By the time she heard Reid leaving the bathroom, she had organised her belongings. As it would be a few more minutes before he was dressed and ready to go, she decided to brush her teeth.

He had left the bathroom immaculate, the dampness of the shower curtain the only clue that someone had used it recently. There was no condensation on the tiles or the mirror so he must have had a cold shower. She hoped that had been from choice, not necessity. But a test showed there was no shortage of hot water.

Fran left her door open when she returned to her room and when Reid emerged from his she was ready to leave.

They had both changed their shirts. Reid's hair was still slightly damp, the way it had been the day she lunched with him.

It wasn't far to the cottage. When Fran knocked on the front door, there was a pause before it was opened by a small boy who would have had to stand on tiptoe and stretch to reach the old-fashioned latch. He was wearing a clean yellow tee shirt but nothing else.

'Mummy's busy,' he announced, before shouting over his shoulder, 'It's Franny and the man, Mummy.'

Fran swung him up in her arms and kissed her nephew's peachy cheek. He had obviously just had a bath and was in the process of dressing himself while her sister attended to his sister.

'This is Sam...and this is Mr Kennard.'

'Hello, Sam.' What Reid thought of being greeted by a half-naked child was impossible to guess. In his world, no doubt, children of this age were always immaculately turned out by a Norland-trained nanny.

'Hello.' Sam wasn't shy. He looped an arm round his aunt's neck and gave her companion a considering look before launching a conversation with, 'My sister's having her bath. It's been a helluva day. One damn thing after another and dinner is going to be a total disaster.'

Fran clamped her back teeth together to stop herself laughing. She could see Reid was doing the same.

'I'm sure it won't be. Your mummy's a wonderful cook.' She set him back on his feet. 'You finish getting dressed. I'll show Mr Kennard round till Mummy's ready.'

'OK.' He ran off, flashing his little bare bottom, a sight which made Fran feel broody every time she saw it.

But Reid might not share her feelings. Brought up in a part of the house separate from his parents' quarters, probably sent off to an exclusive preparatory school when he was still in short trousers, he might think the casual way Shelley's children were being raised was slovenly, not to say slummy. But at least he had been amused by Sam parroting Shelley's moan to John.

John, when they came upon him in a corner of the nursery garden, looked as if it had been a 'helluva' day for him too. Fran had never seen him looking so worn, or so sweaty and dirty. But he managed to put on a smile and an affable manner when she introduced his future brother-in-law.

'If you've had a long drive, you'll be ready for a drink,' he said. 'Fran, you know where the booze is. Fix Reid and yourself a reviver. I'll join you as soon as I've finished packing this order.'

'Don't they have any help?' Reid asked, after they were out of earshot.

'Not full time. It's a hard life, but a very satisfying one...more than a lot of people can say about their jobs.'

'That's true.' Something in his tone made her glance questioningly at him, but as usual his expression was hard to read. Perhaps she had only imagined a note of...what? She couldn't identify what she thought she had heard.

Built on to the back of the cottage was a sizeable conservatory which was the family's main living room.

'What would you like to drink?' she asked.

'A beer would be good.'

'Sit down. Make yourself comfortable.'

If he didn't like the litter of toys and the general untidiness, that was just too bad, was her thought. This was the way it was for young couples bringing up tinies on a tight budget and running a business that forced Shelley to combine mothering with helping John run the plant nursery. It would do Reid good to see how the other half lived.

It wasn't late when they walked back to The Plough. Fran wondered what Reid had thought of the evening.

He had appeared to enjoy it, but his impeccable manners would have made him pretend to even if he hadn't. She was even more curious to know what her sister had thought of him, but would have to wait till tomorrow to find that out.

'John will sleep soundly tonight,' Reid said, as they strolled past the moonlit churchyard, some of its most ancient gravestones leaning at tipsy angles.

'He was having a problem staying awake, wasn't he? He gets up at five, except on Sundays. His idea of a lie-in is staying in bed until seven. It's not as bad now that the children sleep through the night. It was murder when they were teething. Shelley is praying the new baby will be a dormouse.'

'Why don't they put them to bed early and have some time to themselves?' Reid asked. 'It's not as if John is away from home all day like most fathers.'

Fran had often thought the same thing and Gran, who held strong views on the modern way of rearing children, had often lectured Shelley about making a rod for her own back by letting the children stay up until they felt sleepy.

'I don't know. I haven't asked. I don't like being told what to do and I don't suppose Shelley does either. I think she manages brilliantly. Far from being a disaster, the lasagne was delicious. Considering how hard up they are, it's amazing how well she dresses herself and Sam and Emma.'

Because her sister had always discouraged too much help from her family, virtually everything they wore came from charity shops, but Reid wasn't to know that. In his milieu, people supplied the charity shops. They didn't buy from them. Perhaps someone a bit eccentric like Mrs Heatherley might buy something from them occasionally, but Lady Kennard and Mrs Onslow wouldn't be seen dead in other people's discards.

'Yes, your sister's the best asset John could have,'

Reid agreed. 'But on nights when he's not as bushed as he was this evening, I'm sure he'd enjoy exclusive rights to her company. I know I shall when we get to that stage.'

For reasons she hadn't yet analysed, the evening had been a stressful one—and the stress wasn't over yet. There was still a pass to be dealt with…if an attempt by a man to coax his soon-to-be wife to spend the night in his bed could be fairly described as a pass.

A lot of men—and an equal number of women— would regard sleeping together, this close to the wedding, as par for the course. She would herself…if he loved her, if this were a normal engagement. But he didn't, it wasn't and she was torn between curiosity and reluctance; an uncomfortable state of mind which made her sound more belligerent than she intended to be.

'If you think I'm going to hand my babies over to a nanny, think again.'

'I wouldn't suggest that you hand *our* offspring over to anyone,' Reid said calmly. 'But if families can afford it, and if the husband's job involves a good deal of travelling, it makes more sense to have a properly trained nanny than a series of untrained au pair girls. It's also a big advantage to have someone really reliable, whom the children know and like, to baby-sit, rather than being dependent on local teenagers as John and Shelley are…or will be when the business leaves them more time and energy for going out together.'

'I don't think either of them miss a rich full social life. They had it when they were single and now they've moved on to other pleasures. Is your social life very important to you?'

'If you mean the London and New York dinner party circuits—no. Seeing my close friends and making new contacts with people who share my interests—yes. When people marry or even move in together, it's a radical change of lifestyle…can't be otherwise. They have to make major adjustments...sometimes giving up some previous friendships or interests. Whatever happens they need to spend quality time together. That's not easy to do with children demanding their attention.'

'Well, I'm sorry if having Sam and Emma around was a pain as far as you were concerned. It wasn't for the rest of us.' She quickened her pace, knowing she was very close to picking a quarrel but unable to stop herself.

'I didn't say that, or mean it.' Reid's tone was mild but held a hint of impatience.

In fact, as she had to acknowledge, he had been very sweet with both children. When Emma had crawled over to him and hauled herself upright by grasping handfuls of trouser leg in podgy and possibly sticky little fists, he had picked her up and set her astride one long thigh. He hadn't gone as far as to pull silly faces or make baby-speak noises. But he'd let her play with his fingers while holding her firmly in place with his other hand, the sinewy strength of it emphasised by her smallness.

At the time Fran had thought it odd that Reid's hands actually looked stronger than her brother-in-law's, although John did heavy outdoor work and Reid's most strenuous activities appeared to be occasional stints of skiing and windsurfing.

They walked in silence for the rest of the way. In times gone by, when the village houses were lit by oil lamps and candles, most of their inhabitants would have been asleep at this hour. Now nearly all the downstairs windows showed that people were watching TV. A lot of the upstairs windows were also alight as the young of the village watched their own favourite programmes, or played computer games.

Near the pub, a group of late-teens youths and girls were chatting and horsing around. They looked curiously at the strangers. Fran half expected some cheeky remarks to be passed. But perhaps Reid gave the impression that, unlike many people nowadays, he wouldn't tolerate insolence.

The pub was still serving customers. 'Another drink?' he suggested.

'Not for me, but don't let that stop you. I think I'll have a bath.'

'Have you something to read in bed?'

'Yes, thanks. Goodnight, Reid.' While there was friction between them, lifting her cheek seemed out of order. Instead she held out her hand, although that seemed unnaturally formal.

'Goodnight, Francesca.' He lifted her hand to brush his lips against the side of her wrist.

For a moment she was tempted to apologise for her crossness, but thought better of it. As things stood he wasn't likely to try his luck later, after she'd had her bath.

She turned and went up the stairs.

Reid went into the lounge, asked for a double whisky with soda and took it to a corner table.

It had been an interesting evening. He liked Fran's sister and was impressed by her husband, but he thought both children should have been tucked up in bed before supper started. Although the lasagne had been tasty, the vegetables fresh from the garden and the supermarket plonk perfectly drinkable, the meal hadn't been a relaxed one.

He and John hadn't had any problems getting along. But both girls had been on edge. Probably Shelley had been tense because she didn't entertain often enough to be laid-back about it. She had a lot on her plate: what could be a full-time job helping her husband, two energetic tots to cope with and another baby due in a couple of months.

The reason for Fran being strung up was harder to judge. She had kept her tension under control at the cottage, letting some of it out while they were walking back. Spoiling for fight was the phrase that sprang to mind. The antithesis of the urge he was having trouble with.

He sipped his whisky and thought of her lying in the bath, the warm water calming her nerves and sensitising the beautiful creamy skin that went with her fiery hair and emerald-bright eyes. He remembered the lovely shape of her bare back, seen in London the previous afternoon. If the rest of her body was like that...

Fran was standing up in the bath, drying her upper half while the water gurgled down the waste pipe.

The round of pre-nuptial visits was nearly over, thank God. It couldn't ever be easy even in conventional circumstances. One heard and read about in-laws who hated each other on sight. Apart from Mrs Heatherley and her mother, who had horticulture in common, that was likely to be the case with Reid's family and hers.

Careful to leave the bathroom as immaculate as Reid had, she wrapped the damp towel round her sarong-fashion and unlocked the door.

As she stepped onto the landing, lit by a rose-shaded wall lamp, Reid's dark head and broad shoulders appeared on the last but one flight.

She would have had time to dart quickly into her room, but something held her where she was, like a night-roaming rabbit paralysed by the headlamps of an oncoming car.

He turned and came up the last flight, surprisingly light on his feet for such a big man.

'The bathroom's all yours,' she said, conscious that the towel was as short as a micro skirt.

Reid's gaze travelled down to her bare feet and back up to her face. She remembered him saying she turned him on every time she looked at him. She knew he was turned on now.

Did he think she had changed her mind…had lingered in the bathroom until she heard him coming up?

She recovered the power to move, but as she turned, he said, 'Wait…'

CHAPTER FIVE

IT HAD a peremptory ring, suggesting that, if she didn't, she would regret it.

Part of her resented that tone. Another, more amenable side of her nature reminded her she had snapped at him earlier. She could hardly expect to be wooed with soft words after flaring at him like a termagant.

'The bare boards in your room may have splinters. If you haven't brought any slippers, you'd better borrow mine. They'll be too big but better than nothing.'

He opened the door of his room, went inside and almost at once reappeared with a pair of the paper mules which were often among the freebies in luxurious hotels.

'But what about you?' she said, as he placed them on the floor in front of her.

'My soles are harder than yours. Goodnight.' Seconds later she was staring at his closed door.

When she tapped on it next morning, there was no reply. She tapped again. Silence. She opened the door and looked in. The room was empty.

Unless he had plumped up the pillow and smoothed the undersheet, which didn't seem very likely, he had slept more soundly than she had.

She went downstairs and found him already at breakfast in a small room at the back of the building. He rose as she joined him. 'Good morning. Sleep well?'

'Not very.'

'Oh…why was that?'

'I had a guilty conscience.'

'What about?'

'I bit your head off last night…when we were walking back. It wasn't justified. I'm sorry.'

Reid moved his chair further away from the table, sat down and beckoned her to him.

Not sure what he had in mind, she obeyed the gesture. He pulled her onto his lap. 'How about taking a leaf out of Sam's book?'

The night before the little boy had accidentally clouted his sister. Before she could start to wail, he had quickly said, 'Sorry, Emma,' and given her a kiss.

Fran was surprised Reid had noticed. Smiling, she said, 'Sorry, Reid,' and planted a kiss on his temple, the place where her nephew had kissed his sister.

But it didn't end there. He took over, kissing her on the mouth in a way that sent her insides into a high-speed skid.

'Here you are, Mr Kennard.'

When the landlady brought his cooked breakfast, Fran would have leapt off his lap, but he wouldn't let her. Breaking off the kiss, apparently unembarrassed, he said, 'Thank you, Mrs Field. That looks excellent. This is old-fashioned bacon, Fran. Not the factory-farmed stuff. Are you going to have some?'

No longer held, Fran stood up. 'Yes, please. But only one rasher and one egg for me, Mrs Field.'

'Right you are. Coming up.' Beaming, the landlord's wife bustled back to her kitchen.

'Why are you blushing?' said Reid, as Fran took her place opposite. 'I'm sure she's noticed your ring. She's probably wondering why we're in separate rooms. Was that Shelley's idea? Or yours?'

'Shelley asked,' Fran admitted. 'I also made it clear we would be paying the bill. Even at Mrs Field's rates, she and John can't afford it. Their resources are stretched to the limit.'

'I wonder if they need advice on the financial side of things? It's extraordinary how many people don't make the best use of their funds,' Reid said thoughtfully. 'Do you think John would be offended if I brought up the subject and asked a few leading questions?'

'I should think he'd be very pleased to have some expert advice. I know he's not keen on the book-keeping side of the business. Neither of them is. It has to be dealt with, but they both prefer hands-on horticulture.'

After breakfast they returned to the cottage for another couple of hours there before driving on to spend a night with Gran.

After Shelley had made coffee for them, Reid asked if John would mind giving him a guided tour of the whole nursery. Sam went with them and Shelley put Emma in her playpen.

'She doesn't mind being caged when Sam's not around but howls to be free if he is.'

When she was sure the men were well out of earshot, Fran said, 'What do you think of him? What did John say about him?'

'If I weren't happily married, I'd be fighting you for him,' said her sister. 'John likes him too.'

'Do you think Gran will?'

'Of course. Wouldn't anyone? What I want to know is when, where and how it happened. Can I try on that gorgeous ring?'

'Of course.' Fran passed it across. She had already rehearsed answers to all the questions her sister might ask which would skirt round the truth without requiring any seriously black lies.

'Reid wants to get married right away. Do you think that's madness?' she asked.

'If you've made up your minds, why wait?' was Shelley's response. 'If it's going to come unstuck, waiting won't make any difference. John and I knew the day we met that we were right for each other. We had to wait almost a year because there were practical obstacles. That doesn't apply with you and Reid. This is a fabulous ring. He must be a millionaire...or as near as.'

Fran made no comment. To her relief, her sister hadn't, as yet, made the connection between Reid's wealth and the sudden upturn in their mother's circumstances. With luck, she never would.

'Did you give John some advice?' she asked Reid, as they were leaving the village, heading for the northbound motorway.

'Not yet. His basic problem is lack of cash. Sensibly, he doesn't want to take on large loans, but he can't make a lot of progress without new equipment. Perhaps I can steer some venture capital in his direction. Did you have a good gas with your sister?'

'Yes. We squabbled a lot in our teens but now we get on very well.'

At lunchtime they stopped for a snack at a roadhouse but didn't eat much because Fran knew that Gran would expect them to do full justice to her north-country cooking.

Mrs Webb lived in a bungalow bought for her by her late son-in-law at the height of his prosperity when the small terrace house she had lived in since she was married was due to be pulled down to make way for a new development.

The bungalow had an unused garage she had left open so that Reid could drive straight in. He had scarcely switched off the engine before she was there to greet them with a warm embrace for her granddaughter and a handshake accompanied by a beady-eyed scrutiny for Reid.

'I could get a stiff neck looking up at you, lad.' She was only five feet two, her portly figure held firmly in place by a corselet under a floral dress from her favourite mail order company. 'Come in and sit yourself down so that we're more on a level. Kettle's on and I've made

some Fat Rascals; they're one of my Yorkshire specialities,' she told him. Then, looking at her granddaughter, 'She's too thin. I don't think she eats properly, except when she's staying with me.'

'She ate very well last night…we both did,' he told
her. 'Your other granddaughter is an excellent cook.'

'Of course she is, lad, I taught her. You won't need
to go to the expense of having a wedding cake made.
Outrageous the prices they charge for a three-tier cake
these days. I'll bake it and ice it myself and no one will
know the difference.'

'It's sweet of you to offer, Gran, but we aren't having
that sort of wedding,' said Fran, as they entered the
house.

Her grandmother stopped short and stiffened. 'What
do you mean?'

'Reid wants us to get married very quickly and quietly…in a register office.'

'Oh, he does, does he?' Mrs Webb cast him a baleful
look before marching into her kitchen. 'You two go into
the front room, I won't be more than a minute.'

What, from the habit of years, she still termed her
front room, was actually a large lounge with picture windows veiled by lace-edged net curtains whose whiteness
was a matter of deep satisfaction to her.

'As it's your idea, it's up to you to persuade her that
it's a good one,' Fran told Reid in a whisper.

Amazingly he did. From the moment he went to the
kitchen to carry a laden tray for her, until half an hour
later when he let himself be persuaded to eat a third Fat
Rascal, Reid exerted a combination of charm and psychological insight that it was awesome to watch.

By the time tea was cleared away, he had Gran eating
out of his hand. But she had some tricks of her own.

'While we're doing the washing up, do me a favour,
would you, lad? The post box is just down the road.
Turn right from the gate. I meant to pop down with this

letter. It won't go tonight but it will go first thing to-morrow.'

Having got rid of him, and Fran wouldn't put it past her to have written the letter for precisely that purpose, she said, 'Your mother told me he was nice. Daphne's no judge of character but for once she was right. I took to him straight away. He'll suit you a darn sight better than that other young fellow.'

Fran gave the old lady a sharp look. 'What other young fellow?'

'You might be able to pull the wool over your mother's and your sister's eyes, but you can't fool me,' said her grandmother. 'I always knew you had a yen for the chauffeur's son. Never could see what you saw in him. But there you are, teenage girls do have these silly crushes. I did myself, more's the pity. I hoped you'd grow out of yours, and you have, thank goodness. This big lad will suit you much better than that weedy Julian. All brains and no balls, he was.'

Fran was torn between wanting to laugh at Gran's typically pithy character assassination and a lingering instinct to protest that it wasn't true. Julian had more than brains to recommend him. But she didn't in case Gran suspected her of agreeing to marry Reid on the rebound.

'I had no idea you guessed how I felt about Julian.'

'There's an old saying "The onlooker sees most of the game",' said Gran. 'You're very like I was at your age, except you've had more advantages. At fourteen you were in love with love, the same way I was. Like a fool, I married my first love and lived to regret it. Yours married someone else, leaving you free to find someone a lot more suitable.'

'You've only just met him. How do you know he's more suitable?'

'When you get to my age you can recognise a good 'un...or a bad 'un,' said the old lady. 'I'm not saying the chauffeur's lad was a bad 'un. I dare say he'll do very well…end up a professor most likely. But he wasn't man enough to keep you in order.'

'I don't want to be kept in order, Gran. Marriage should be a partnership between equals.'

'That's as may be.' Mrs Webb put the last saucer in the plastic rack on the draining board. 'I was married for thirty years to a man who was weaker than I was. I knew it, he knew it and it made trouble between us. You won't have that problem with Reid.'

'I hope I won't have any problems with Reid.'

'You're bound to have some. Two strong-minded people can't set up house together without a few wrangles. Up to now you've had it all your own way. Your dad gave you everything you asked for. Your mother never said boo to a goose. It's a wonder they didn't spoil you. I reckon you can thank me for that…me and the teachers at that school I made them send you to. You've turned out well, you and Shelley, but you need someone stronger than her John. Someone a bit more exciting.'

'There's nothing very thrilling about banking,' said Fran. 'I think it's a dull occupation.'

'No duller than being a mathematician like Julian.' As Fran finished drying the dishes, Mrs Webb lifted the plate rack to wipe the drainer. 'Though I will agree Reid doesn't look like a banker. He strikes me as more like those fellows who sail round the world in yachts, or run safari parks in Africa. I can't see him behind a desk. Is he happy at it?'

'I suppose so. I haven't asked him.'

Mrs Webb looked scandalised. 'You're wearing his ring and you don't know whether he's happy at his work? It's high time you did, girl. That's your mission in life from now on…making sure he's a happy man.'

'Presumably if he wasn't he wouldn't be doing it. Your ideas about marriage are a bit old-fashioned, Gran. These days making it work isn't all down to the woman.'

'Never was, love,' Gran said firmly. 'A good marriage is two people wanting the best for each other and moving heaven and earth to make damn sure they get it.'

'I know Reid wants several children. We both do.'

'Children don't make a marriage. They're on loan to you for a few years, then they go off and make their own lives. It's the two of you, loving each other, that's the important part.'

This was the edge of a minefield. Anxious to skirt it, Fran said, 'How did you know how I loved Julian? No one else did, not even Shelley.'

'No, you hid it from everyone but your old gran…and just as well, the way matters turned out. Julian would have felt awkward having you at the wedding if he'd known the way you felt about him. I was proud of you that day, Franny. You put on a brave face and never let anyone know how unhappy you felt. Still, it was all for the best. You—' She broke off as Reid walked past the window and came in by the back door.

The upper part of the window was open. Had he heard what was being said? Would he want to know the cause of her unhappiness?

His face gave nothing away. He said, 'Your garden is very well kept, Mrs Webb. Do you do it yourself?'

'You may be a wizard at high finance, Reid, but you obviously have no idea what jobbing gardeners charge these days. I can't bend as well as I could, but I'll go on doing my own garden until they cart me off to an old people's home. And I'll have to be in a bad way before I let them do that,' she added tartly.

The bungalow had three bedrooms. That night Reid slept in the spare double room and Fran in the very small single. She lay awake, thinking about him with his head only inches from hers on the other side of the wall behind the headboard.

Very soon their heads would be side by side on adjoining pillows, or even sharing the same pillow. She found it easier to visualise Julian and Alice doing that than herself and Reid.

The discovery that Gran had always known about her feelings for Julian had been upsetting. What Gran didn't know and, hopefully, never would was that although Fran had renounced those feelings and tried never to think of him, sometimes thoughts, such as the one she had just had, slipped through her guard. And when they did she knew that loving someone was far, far harder to stop than habits like biting one's nails or smoking, neither of which she had ever done herself but which she'd seen other people struggle to overcome. Perhaps the only cure for an old love was a new love.

But even if she could love Reid, he didn't want that. Learning to love him would only lead to greater unhappiness.

At breakfast next morning, Gran said, 'As you're denying my granddaughter her big day, I hope you're intending to give her a slap-up honeymoon.'

Reid was spreading some of her home-made marmalade on a piece of toast. Smiling at her, he said, 'I wouldn't deny Francesca anything that she really wanted, Mrs. Webb. She agreed that a quiet wedding would be more appropriate and less stressful for her mother after being recently widowed.'

'There's that to it, I suppose,' Mrs Webb conceded grudgingly. 'But I do enjoy a nice wedding and I shan't be here by the time little Emma gets wed.'

'I should think you probably will be, Gran. Great-Granny was still around in her nineties, wasn't she?'

'Aye, and she'd had a hard life. Where do you think you might go…for your honeymoon, I mean?'

'We haven't discussed it yet. We'll talk about it today,' said Reid, effectively closing any further immediate discussion.

As Fran had noticed before, he was good at erecting

trespass-proof fences around matters he felt were not in the public domain. It was a useful technique, especially with people like Gran whose interest, though well-meant, could sometimes be intrusive. But would some of his innermost thoughts always remain closed off, even from his wife?

'Where would you like to honeymoon?' he asked, when they were on their way again. 'A favourite place you'd like to go back to? Somewhere neither of us has been before?'

Fran cast her mind over the places she'd visited with her mother and with friends. She'd enjoyed them at the time but none of them beckoned her back. Wherever they went, for a couple who weren't in love a honeymoon was bound to be something of an ordeal. Of course people who weren't in love but fancied each other like mad went on holiday together and had a great time. But usually the female partner had a lot more experience than she had.

After a pause, she said, 'I think I'd like you to surprise me.'

'Really?' He took his eyes off the road for a second to give her a searching look. 'Are you sure about that?'

'I'm sure you're capable of organising a magical mystery honeymoon,' she said airily.

'No problem,' he agreed. 'That's something else settled, then...at least as far as you're concerned. I'll try not to disappoint you.'

Had they been a normal couple, it would have been her cue to say, 'Darling, wherever we go will be bliss because we'll be together.'

Instead she said lightly, 'I've always liked surprises. By the way, I'd like to read your investigator's report on me. Is there any reason why I shouldn't see it?'

'None at all. I'll have a copy sent to you.'

After bringing her home, Reid didn't suggest extend-

ing their time together by staying the night before returning to London.

Within an hour of arriving, he was back in the car.
Watching him drive away, Fran felt that his goodbye kiss
had been almost perfunctory, as if having done what was
necessary to bring matters to the point of a public announcement, his mind was now on other things which
had nothing to do with her.

The announcement was in the 'Forthcoming Marriages'
column of two of the serious newspapers next day.

Fran's mother cut them out and pasted them in one
of the two albums she had bought long ago to record the
major events in her daughters' lives.

During the morning an express courier service deliv-
ered a package. Fortunately Fran saw it coming from her
bedroom window and ran downstairs, calling to Janie
that she would answer the door.

She took the package back to her room and read it in
private. Much of the information the investigator had
unearthed was similar to the stuff in her mother's album.
Not surprisingly, his report said she had been 'extremely
discreet' in her relationships with members of the opposite sex. He had dug up quite a lot of clippings showing her as a bridesmaid at friends' weddings or attending
fashionable parties, but always laughing and chatting
with other women, never tête-à-tête with a man. 'In
London Ms Turner frequents fashionable shops and
smart restaurants,' he had noted.

The report went into considerable detail about her parents and grandparents, so Reid had been under no illu-
sions about her family background when he summoned
her to his presence.

The most surprisingly item was a quote from the head-
mistress of her school. 'Francesca didn't always make
the best of her time here and, academically, her achievements fell considerably short of our hopes for her. But

she left us with the impression that, once she had found her *métier*, she would do well and become a useful and resourceful member of society.'

How on earth had the author of the report managed to extract that comment from the formidable Miss Watson? Fran wondered. And why 'resourceful'? Although she knew the word's meaning, looking it up in the dictionary for a more exact definition, she found 'ingenious, capable, and full of initiative, esp. in dealing with difficult situations.'

But it hadn't been her initiative which had resolved the difficulties following her father's bankruptcy and death, she thought wryly. All she had done in that situation was to grasp the solution offered to her. There was nothing resourceful about that, except in the sense that it took a degree of nerve to grab such a desperate solution. Although there were plenty of women who wouldn't regard marriage to a rich man who was neither too old for her nor physically repulsive as much of a penance.

At Reid's suggestion, she went to London again the following week, ostensibly to buy her wedding outfit and trousseau. Actually she went to see him, only to find he had gone to a meeting in Brussels and she was alone with Lady Kennard, Mrs Onslow being in the country with one of her daughters who had just had a baby.

'I was going down to Devon, but I thought you might not care for being here on your own,' Lady Kennard said graciously. In fact Fran would have preferred it. She could have spent hours in Reid's book room, getting to know his library, instead of being forced to take part in conversations designed to make her feel an unworthy addition to the Kennard dynasty.

She bore it as best she could but dug her heels in when Lady K suggested accompanying her on shopping forays. Fran had decided to wear something she already owned and only to buy some glamorous underwear.

On her second night in London, Reid returned, surprised and possibly displeased to find his grandmother still in residence.

After dinner, he asked her to excuse them which left her looking put out while they went up to the book room.

'How have you been getting on?' he asked, on the way upstairs.

'Fine,' she said brightly. 'As you know from the report on me, shopping is one of my favourite occupations.'

He smiled and reached for her hand. 'Then you should be in a good mood, but I sense that you're not. Having cold feet?'

The clasp of his long strong fingers should have been reassuring, but somehow it wasn't.

'Can you honestly say you don't have any doubts?'

'If I had I would call it off. You don't *have* to go through with this, Francesca. If you really feel you can't face it...' He left the sentence unfinished.

Instead of answering that, she said, 'I want to know why you chose me. There has to be more to it than the reasons you've given so far.'

He released her hand and was silent until they were in the book room. Closing the door, he gestured for her to be seated on one of the sofas. But instead of joining her there, he sat down on the other one. For the first time in their acquaintance he looked a little worn and she wondered about the business that had taken him to Brussels and whether the trip had been successful.

'When you belong to a family like mine, you have special responsibilities. You start learning about them early. I grew up accepting that, eventually, an accumulation of tradition would rest on my shoulders. From a long way back, the Kennards have always married the daughters of other banking families.'

Suddenly he sprang to his feet and began to pace about the room. 'I think it's time to introduce some fresh genes into our bloodline. Your father started from nothing and was extremely successful until he overreached himself. I admire him for that. The chances are that his driving force will jump a generation and motivate the children we have.'

'Couldn't you have found someone with driving force whose daughters did better at school than I did?'

'The qualities that make a head girl or a games captain aren't necessarily what a man looks for in his wife. You have other attributes.' His hard eyes appraised her figure and legs. 'Come over here...'

Fran wasn't sure she liked being spoken to in an authoritative tone which took it for granted she would obey his command. At the same time something within her was excited by his dominance.

She rose and crossed to the other sofa, intending to sit beside him but finding herself drawn onto his lap.

Unlike that of many tall men, Reid's height wasn't mostly in the length of his legs or in an extra-long torso. She had noticed during their round of family visits that he was in perfect proportion. Usually she had to look up at him. Now, sitting on his thighs, she found their eye-levels almost matched.

'I've just spent forty-eight hours surrounded by powermongers, mostly male. It's a relaxing change to be alone with someone delectably female.' He laid one arm across her legs while his other hand moved up her back to bury itself in her hair. 'Tell me about your shopping. What did you buy?'

'Things to wear wherever it is that we're going. But don't worry, I'm not a person who packs for every conceivable eventuality and routinely exceeds their baggage allowance. I travel as lightly as possible and fill any gaps when I get there.' She was aware, as she spoke, that it wasn't easy to keep her mind on what she was saying. Her brain seemed to be closing down leaving only her senses functioning.

'Good. That's my system too. I rarely take more than a suit bag and a flight bag.'

She had the feeling that Reid was also on autopilot, the focus of his thoughts quite different from what he was talking about. His right hand was lightly caressing her hip, his left hand shaped to the back of her head with the tip of his thumb moving gently in the soft crevice behind her ear. She knew that very soon now he was going to kiss her. She had the feeling that though he had promised to respect the condition she had set the last time they were in this room, the kiss might still go a lot further than any of his previous kisses.

The next moment two things happened. The telephone started to ring and, at the very same instant, she became aware of his body's involuntary response to their closeness.

Reid muttered an angry expletive but he didn't attempt to restrain her when she jumped up to allow him to take the call. The telephone was on one of the end tables flanking the other sofa.

Calls to the Kennards' number listed in the telephone directory were answered by Curtis, the butler. Reid had given her the ex-directory number for the extensions in his part of the house and also his mobile number.

Whoever was calling had to be on close terms with him. She could also hear that the voice which spoke after his curt 'Hello' was feminine.

Wondering if their embrace had been aborted by one of his former girlfriends, Fran listened to his side of the conversation. Soon it was clear that the caller was someone wanting to know why they hadn't been asked to the wedding. Which seemed to rule out his old flames.

While listening to a long and indignant-sounding statement by the caller, Reid leaned back and closed his eyes, his lips compressed with contained exasperation.

Fran found herself wondering what he would do if, while he was still on the phone, she went over, snuggled up beside him and did something sexy like nibbling the lobe of his ear or running her palm over his washboard midriff. She realised she was longing to see the body beneath the international businessman's uniform of expensive bespoke suit and shirt.

She had first seen Julian's body when he was fifteen and she was ten, swimming in the Turners' pool the first summer after her father engaged Jack Wallace as his chauffeur. Julian had been skinny then but had filled out quite a lot since. He certainly wasn't anything like a cartoonist's idea of an academic, four-eyed and round-shouldered. But at no time when they had been alone together had she felt impelled to unbutton his shirt and slip her hand inside to explore his chest: an impulse she had felt more than once in Reid's company.

He said goodbye to the caller and replaced the receiver. But he didn't beckon Fran back to his lap. Instead, standing up, he said, 'As you'll have gathered, that was one of my cousins wanting to know why we're having a quiet wedding. I'm feeling a bit bushed tonight. If you don't mind, I'll turn in early.'

'Of course not.' He did look tired, but not *that* tired. A few moments ago he had been ready to make love. Clearly it was an excuse to avoid the temptation to go back on his promise.

They returned to the landing, said goodnight and went in different directions.

With her grandmother, mother and sister—but not John who had to stay at home with the children—Fran spent the night before her wedding in a hotel suite booked for them by Reid's secretary.

They had dinner in the hotel restaurant.

'So we shan't be meeting his family till after the wedding,' said Gran, with a disapproving sniff. 'If it had been *my* grandson getting wed, and his bride-to-be's family having to do all the travelling, I'd have laid on a welcome at my house, small as it is. It seems like his side of the family don't want to know about our side.'

'We're their guests here, Mum,' said Fran's mother. 'This is a lovely hotel but the flowers in our rooms are an extra. That was a very thoughtful touch.'

'We're not invited to the house. Where I come from that's next door to telling you straight you're not wanted.'

'That's nonsense, Gran,' Fran said firmly, although in her heart she felt there was a good deal of truth in the old lady's allegation, especially as far as Lady Kennard was concerned. Gran's grammatical mistakes and north-country expressions wouldn't go down at all well with that arch-snob. They wouldn't matter to Mrs Heatherley. She would judge people by the warmth of their hearts, their capacity for kindness.

'Lady Kennard is older than you are and she doesn't have your energy,' she continued. 'Having the wedding lunch here will be less of a strain for her.'

'I thought you said she had a butler and other staff? It would have been them doing the work, not her lady-ship.'

'Yes, but it's still very stressful, having the reception at home, Mum,' put in her daughter.

'Eight people! You call that a reception?' Gran was in one of her tetchy moods.

She went on niggling until Fran, exasperated, said, 'You're upsetting me, Gran. Getting married is nerve-racking enough without you finding fault with every-thing. Tomorrow is my big day…even if it's different from your idea of a wedding. Can we please talk about something else?'

Later, while she was getting ready for bed in the twin-bedded room she was sharing with her sister while the others were in single rooms on the far side of the sitting room, Shelley said, 'When you said getting married was nerve-racking, you were only trying to make Gran shut up, weren't you, Franny? You aren't really jittery, are you?'

'Isn't that normal with brides? Weren't you, the night before you married John?'

'I was in bed with John,' her sister said, with a grin. 'We'd been making love whenever we had the chance. When everyone else was in bed, I sneaked out and joined him in his room. His parents were in the room next to his, so we had to be as quiet as mice. It was actually better than the next night when I was tired from being on show all day. Big weddings are fun for the guests, but they're a terrific strain on the couple getting married. No matter what Gran thinks about it, I reckon you and Reid have got it right. When you get to wherever you're going, you'll be in much better shape than John and I were. Although he hadn't had a stag night, I remember him saying on the plane that he felt totally knackered...not the ideal state for a bridegroom.'

Fran laughed, which she knew was her sister's intention.

Not wanting Shelley to know how worried she felt, she said, in a cheerful tone, 'I wonder where we are going? I've packed a swimsuit and a beach wrap, with my cashmere shawl in case it's a place where it gets cold after dark.'

'I wonder if it'll be overtly ritzy, or one of those resorts I've read about where the visitors are all seriously rich but like to play Robinson Crusoe in a thatched hut with all mod cons and miles of perfect private beach?' Shelley speculated.

'Who knows? Reid's idea of a perfect honeymoon place could be game fishing, or something equally way-out. Maybe it was a bit reckless to give him carte blanche.'

'As long as it isn't bungee jumping. That's one of John's madder ambitions,' said Shelley, pulling a face.

'Anyway this time tomorrow night you should know the worst...or the best.'

In more senses than one, was Fran's thought.

They went on talking for a while after they'd put the lights out. Then Fran, wide awake, said something and got no reply. Her sister had gone to sleep.

She gave a deep sigh, longing for sleep to blot out the turmoil going on in her mind. She reminded herself that in many parts of the world people married for other reasons than love and, on balance, it seemed to work out just as well as it did in the countries where love was considered the best, the only motivation.

But it still felt as if, tomorrow, she would be committing herself to a bond which had more chance of going wrong than going right.

CHAPTER SIX

FRAN'S wedding outfit had been bought for evening parties. It consisted of a short-waisted jacket of white silk gabardine over a crêpe de Chine chemise with a flaring white chiffon skirt. Like the edges of expensive Christmas ribbons, the hand-rolled hem of the skirt had a fine wire threaded through it, making the filmy fabric form undulating ripples. It was the pretty frothy hem that had prompted an impulse buy, the last one before her father's crash.

To go with it, instead of white shoes, she had chosen a pair of pale grey sling-backs and a small matching clutch purse. Palest grey lace-topped stay-ups made her feel ultra-feminine.

She had decided to ignore the traditional 'something old…something borrowed, something blue' as being inappropriately sentimental for this particular wedding.

In her ears and round her neck she intended to wear the discreet cultured pearls chosen by her mother for her sixteenth birthday. At the time Fran had thought them boringly demure. At that age she had been into bold kooky pieces. Now that she had outgrown the fashion victim phase, she wore the pearls more often.

They were all having breakfast in bed and when the floor waiter wheeled in their trays, on Fran's there was a parcel.

'From Reid of course,' said Shelley, when her sister wondered aloud where it could have come from.

She was right. Inside a satin-lined leather case was a necklace composed of many strands of small matched dark green beads, clasped by a carved oval of paler green

97

stone. The matching earrings were a combination of the two colours. With them was a card with the jeweller's name engraved in small gold type at the top and a handwritten message below.

I hope these will please you. R

The initial consisted of a thick bold upward slash and a thinner downstroke with a long flowing tail.

'Gran will say green is unlucky,' said Fran, putting the breakfast tray aside and throwing back the bedclothes to go to the dressing table.

'They're nice, but I thought he would give you diamonds,' said Shelley.

Fran had spent more time looking in the windows of the leading jewellers than her sister. The name on the card was arguably the most exclusive establishment in Bond Street.

'The beads are emeralds and the clasp is jade, probably antique and probably madly valuable,' she said dryly.

The skein of beads made a cool collar round the base of her throat. The beautiful clasp made it possible to wear it in several ways, with the clasp at the front or resting on one of her collarbones.

It looked incongruous with the long T-shirt she was leaving for her mother to take home. But it would look wonderful with her white outfit. She replaced the jewellery in its box and went back to bed to drink her orange juice and eat a kipper followed by toast and marmalade.

Shelley was ready before her and, sensing that her sister would like some time to herself, joined the others in the sitting room while Fran was still putting the finishing touches to her light make-up. As usual, she had done her hair herself, not wishing to let a strange hairdresser loose on it.

The white outfit had looked good with her pearls. With Reid's emeralds it looked fabulous. She knew she had never and would never look better than she did today, her appearance of confident elegance at odds with the profound unease inside her.

When she walked into the sitting room, her mother burst into tears.

'For goodness' sake, Daphne...' Gran expostulated impatiently. But her own eyes were suspiciously bright as she looked at her younger grandchild who had grown up so tall and poised and was making a brilliant marriage.

'You look drop-dead gorgeous,' said Shelley, faintly surprised to see that her sister wasn't wearing a hat or any form of headdress.

Very soon they were all in the huge limousine taking them to the register office where there was no sign of the bridegroom's relations but he was waiting on the pavement, looking especially debonair in a grey suit, white shirt and an apricot tie with an apricot rose in his buttonhole.

With the driver holding the door and Reid ready to assist them, the others climbed out first and had their hands kissed, probably the first time it had ever happened to them, thought Fran, watching.

Then it was her turn to follow. As she stepped onto the pavement, Reid brought from behind his back a small exquisite posy of old-fashioned Parma violets.

'Good morning, Francesca.'

The formality of his greeting was at variance with the appreciative gleam in his eyes as they appraised her.

She put the flowers to her nose, inhaling a fragrance redolent of a more gracious era. As she did so, she realised they were held by something she recognised as a small silver posy holder, probably Edwardian or Victorian.

'How pretty...thank you.' She added, 'And thank you for these,' touching the emerald beads. 'I have a memento for you, but I'll give it to you later.'

The three other guests were waiting for them inside and Reid performed the introductions. Then it was time for the ceremony.

Fran had always expected to get married in the country church where Shelley and John had made their vows. The register office ritual had hardly begun before it was over and they were leaving the building to return to the hotel, Reid and herself in the car by themselves, with the others following on.

His first kiss as her husband, in the register office had been a feather-light brush of his mouth against hers. He didn't attempt to repeat it, more warmly, as they drove the short distance back.

'That's a lovely dress,' he told her.

'I think you must be psychic,' said Fran.

When he lifted an enquiring eyebrow, she unbuttoned her jacket and showed him the belt of velvet ribbon round her waist. It was exactly the same colour as the violets.

'Did you choose them yourself?'

'Naturally. Did you think I'd delegate the choice of my bride's flowers to my secretary?'

'No, but you might have asked Mrs Heatherley's advice.'

He shook his head. 'My mother collected small silver objects. The posy holder was one of them. The violets seemed the right colour to go with your hair.'

In the private room where they were having lunch, a large round table was decorated with white flowers and greenery. Fran drank her first glass of champagne quickly, needing the buzz. She was still very strung up.

Although the meal was delicious, starting with a grilled goat's cheese salad followed by poached sea trout with truffle mayonnaise and braised baby shallots, Fran found it hard to do it justice. Lady Kennard, on her left, kept up a non-stop flow of small talk and Gran was doing the same thing on Reid's right.

Fran's mother and Mrs Heatherly were deeply immersed in garden problems and Shelley and Mrs Onslow were talking about babies. Glad that they were enjoying themselves, but longing for it to be over, Fran drank more than she ate, not realising how much until Reid suddenly turned to her and said quietly, 'A little more blotting paper and a little less bubbly might be a good idea.'

It was said in a good-humoured tone and no one else overheard it, but Fran felt deeply embarrassed. It was only then that she realised how assiduously the waiter had been topping up her glass and how unwisely rapidly she had been emptying it, especially as champagne was famous for entering the bloodstream faster than still wines.

When the pudding was served, nectarines marinated in something alcoholic, she knew his warning had been justified and wished she had eaten more bread and new potatoes when she had the chance. It was too late now. She would just have to be extra careful when she stood up.

It was Mrs Heatherley who, in the absence of the customary toasts, suddenly rose to her feet, saying, 'I should like to say a few words. We hear a great deal of talk, both in public and private, about the breakdown of marriage. It's my belief that there never were very many perfect marriages. But they happen and, I believe, will go on happening. I hope many years ahead Reid and Francesca will look back on today as the beginning of one of those strong and satisfying relationships. We all wish them well.'

She raised her glass and smiled across the table at them. 'To Reid and Francesca and their future together.'

The others echoed the toast. As Mrs Heatherley sat down, Reid stood up. 'Thank you, Granny... Thank you,' he said to the rest of the party. 'It's almost time for my wife'—he paused to smile down at her—'to change, so I'll keep this brief. You all know the adage "Marry in haste, repent at leisure". I persuaded Francesca to marry me in haste. I intend to make sure she never repents that decision.'

'Well said, lad.' Mrs Webb began clapping and the others joined in.

Smiling, Reid went on, 'The rest of you may like to stay and talk and perhaps have tea before you leave. But as we're due to take off from Heathrow an hour from now, you'd better get cracking, darling.'

Shelley went upstairs with Fran to pack her wedding clothes for her. They would be left in the care of Lady Kennard.

'Reid's very generous...sending cars to fetch us and take us home,' said Shelley, as Fran undressed down to her new-on-today Italian bra, briefs and satin half slip. 'You're going to be cushioned in luxury from now on, Franny. More so than we were by Dad. He could be a bit mean at times. I'm sure he spent more on his girl-friends than he did on Mum. I can't see her marrying again which is sad really. She's only forty-six. If I'd been her, knowing Dad was unfaithful, I'd have found myself a lover. But Mum would think that was wicked.'

Fran wasn't in the mood to discuss their mother's sex life. Right now she felt envious of her. Tonight, when she went to bed, Mrs Turner would probably spend an hour engrossed in a favourite gardening book from her large collection. Fran herself would be ending the day very differently: in bed with a man who as a lover could be anywhere on the scale from one to ten. From what she had heard from girlfriends about their men, it was risky to assume that because a man was attractive he would be an ace between the sheets.

She put on co-ordinated separates; a dark grape-coloured skirt with a pale lilac silk shirt and an aubergine blazer, the offbeat colours she loved and that set off her hair and also the emerald beads.

'I wonder if I should take these, or leave them in Lady K's care?' she pondered aloud.

'Ask Reid,' Shelley suggested. 'I should think the sort of hotels you'll be staying in will all have safes in the rooms. Most five-star places do.'

When Fran consulted Reid, he said, 'It might be better to leave them behind.'

The farewell embraces took another five minutes and then they went to the waiting car.

'Are you glad that's over or did you enjoy it?' Reid asked, as it glided away from the hotel's palatial entrance.

'Some of it.' She was still smarting slightly from his reproof at the table.

'I hope the photographs are good so that our children can see how beautiful you looked. You have very good taste. I like that outfit too,' he said, looking at it.

'Would you have married me if I'd had dreadful taste?'

'You would still have been you.'

He was very good at diplomatic answers, she thought, and he was doing his best to behave as if this were an ordinary marriage.

She had brought the posy of violets with her. Inside the silver holder, she had discovered, their stems were encased in a small plastic bag with a damp tissue inside it. They reminded her that the time it took to reach the airport was an opportunity to give him the memento in her shoulder bag. She took it out, neatly wrapped in thick brown paper tied with dark green tape sealed with red wax.

'I hope you'll like this. It's my wedding present to you.' She had raised the money to buy it by selling two favourite possessions, an eighteenth-century fan and a portrait miniature of a lady with powdered hair. She had found them in a country antique shop when she was still in her teens and they had appreciated in value. It had seemed important to buy something for him with money she could call her own.

Rather surprisingly, Reid had a Swiss army knife clipped to the back of his belt. It wasn't the sort of accessory she expected a banker to have concealed on his person.

He cut the tape and unfolded the paper, his eyebrows rising as he uncovered a slim leather-bound volume inside. He opened it, reading the title page.

'I've been looking for this for years. How did you know? How did you find it?'

'The head of my school said I was resourceful,' she reminded him.

He turned the pages, glancing at the engravings illustrating the text. Then he closed the book and studied the binding with a lyre stamped in gold on the front. Finally he looked at her, a long intent look that she couldn't interpret.

'You couldn't have given me anything that would have pleased me more. Thank you, Francesca.' He leaned towards her, taking her chin in his free hand and, for the second time that day, kissing her lightly on the lips.

At the check-in desk she found out where they were going from the indicator board behind it.

The last place she would have expected. Bordeaux, in south-west France.

But that couldn't be their final destination. People honeymooned in Paris. It was one of the classic locations. Bordeaux's image was different and much less romantic. It was a major centre of the wine trade, a mecca for connoisseurs of fine wine, a city frequented by shippers of vintage claret.

As the conveyor swept their cases away, Reid insisted on carrying her flight bag as well as his own. They went through Security, Fran showing her new married-name passport. It would take time to get used to being Francesca Kennard. She still felt like Fran Turner. But as Reid preferred to call her Francesca, that was probably how she would be known to the people she met in this new life starting today.

In the public departure lounge they bought magazines for the flight before going to the first-class lounge of the French airline they were flying with. Flying first class wasn't a new experience. She had done it before, many times, but always going somewhere more glamorous than Bordeaux. Predictably, most of the other passengers in the lounge were well-fed middle-aged men with cigar smokers' florid complexions accompanied by middle-aged wives or much younger women with the equally recognisable attributes of the trophy companion.

Very soon it was time to board. As she settled herself in the window seat, Fran remembered the aerial view of a French château in the folder Reid had handed her the first time they met. Perhaps it belonged to him and that was their destination. But she didn't intend to ask.

They were still on the tarmac when a stewardess offered them champagne or orange juice or a mixture of both. Fran chose juice and asked for a glass of water in which to refresh the violets. She had seen people glancing at them but doubted if any one of them guessed that they were, in effect, her bridal bouquet.

They were met at the airport by a driver holding up a placard with 'M. Kennard' printed on it. Travelling with her mother, Fran had always been in charge, doing everything she could to relieve Mrs Turner of the smallest anxiety or effort. Now it was she who was being cosseted.

It wouldn't have surprised her to see nothing of the city but its bypass. Instead it was soon apparent they were heading straight for the centre. Although the rush hour was over, traffic was still heavy and the driving competitive.

Presently they drew up outside a splendid hotel and went through the customary ritual of arrival at such a grand establishment. Very soon they were being ushered into a spacious suite overlooking the hotel's formal garden.

After a conversation in French with a dapper assistant manager, Reid said to her, 'Would you like a maid to unpack for you?'

'No, thank you.'

A pass key rattled in the lock of the door of the adjoining bedroom. Their luggage had arrived. The dapper young man wished them an enjoyable stay in French and English, the baggage porters accepted their tips and closed the door behind them. They were alone.

'I'm going to unpack and change,' said Reid. 'The dining room here is probably fairly formal. Perhaps it would be more relaxing to go out and find a bistro. What do you think?'

'That would be fine with me.'

'Give me your keys and I'll unlock your case.'

Fran handed over her key-ring and watched him deal with the little gold padlock, open the two long zips, and fold back the top of the case.

'Thank you.'

She took off her jacket and began to unpack, conscious that most newly married couples would have been in each other's arms by now, probably on the brink of making love for the first time as Mr and Mrs or Monsieur and Madame. But her husband seemed more interested in distributing his belongings than in claiming the intimate privileges to which he was now entitled.

The fact that he was unpacking everything made it seem that her guess had been wrong. This *was* their destination. As they hung their clothes in the generous closet space, she wondered if he could be cold-blooded enough to combine business with pleasure; expecting her to please him at night but to spend the days on her own while he did deals with the city's leading wine barons.

She was still unpacking when Reid started to change by sitting down in a chair and taking off his black shoes and grey silk socks. He had already shed his tie and now he unbuttoned the cuffs and front of his shirt and pulled it free from his trousers. Although she wasn't watching him doing this, she was aware of his actions out of the corner of her eye.

Weird as it might seem to many of her contemporaries, especially those who, on holiday, had a succession of one-night stands and thought nothing of it, because of Julian she had never been in a room with a man while he was undressing.

Reid emptied his trouser pockets of loose change before unbuckling his belt and unthreading it from the loops of his waistband. The sound of the zip being pulled down, inaudible to anyone with their mind on other things, seemed to Fran as loud as a piece of Velcro being ripped open. She was aware of him stepping out of his trousers and placing the hems together before turning away to hang them up.

For a moment, while his back was turned, she flashed a swift glance at his rear view and felt her insides turn over and her throat constrict. She had guessed from the way he moved that he was much fitter than most City men. But she hadn't been prepared for the muscles rippling like sidewinders all over his broad brown back. She felt an instinctive frisson of fear and fascination.

From a formidable breadth of shoulder, his back narrowed down to a slim waist without an ounce of surplus flesh. A hard male backside was covered by a brief pair of light blue boxer shorts. Below them, his long legs had a naturally elegant shape with the exercised look of a sculler's or a cyclist's thighs and calves. Wherever he went to maintain this level of fitness, he was a walking advertisement for the gym and its machines.

When she looked at him again he was in holiday mode: chinos, a cotton shirt and deck shoes with bare brown ankles. A dark blue blazer was slung over a chair, ready to be shrugged on when they went out.

Fran had decided not to change. What she was wearing might have been a bit formal for a village bistro, but here in Bordeaux it wouldn't look out of place. Also she wasn't ready to take off her clothes in front of him, but to do it in the bathroom might cause some sardonic comment.

'Have you been here before?' she asked, as they left the hotel.

'Yes, many times.' Reid took her elbow before they crossed the street, releasing it when they reached the opposite pavement.

This seemed to confirm her suspicion that he was here on business.

As they strolled through what was clearly a fashionable part of the city, the evening air was many degrees milder than this time yesterday in London. There it still felt like a chilly spring. Here it was early summer with an air temperature that made sitting outside not only possible but enjoyable.

By now the effect of the champagne at lunch had worn off. When a waiter came to take their order for drinks, Fran asked for white wine. Her schoolgirl French was equal to ordering food and drinks but she knew that her accent wasn't as good as Reid's which was why she said what she wanted in English to Reid, rather than speaking to the waiter.

It annoyed her that she lacked the confidence to speak French in front of him. It wasn't like her. Usually she didn't give a damn what anyone thought. Why was she having these silly inhibitions with the man she ought to feel more at ease with than anyone else in the world?

'I wish you would tell me how you managed to find

that first edition,' said Reid, while they were waiting for
the drinks to come.

'It wasn't difficult. I looked up the telephone numbers
of the leading antiquarian booksellers and rang them up
to ask if you were a customer, explaining that we were
going to be married and I wanted to buy a present for
you. I struck lucky with the second call. They couldn't
have been more helpful. It turned out that book had been
offered to them by a provincial dealer just a short time
before I rang.'

'That was enterprising.'

'Not really. I'm a shopping expert. It's the nearest I
come to having a profession,' she told him, smiling.

'I was reading a piece about women and shopping in
the paper the other day. It said compulsive shopping is
a substitute for sex...or, more precisely, satisfying sex.'

'Papers are always running those sorts of pieces. They
all do it. I wouldn't be surprised if the journalist made
it up, or found some obscure psychiatrist who wanted to
get his name in lights.'

As she was speaking, Fran was uncomfortably conscious that, although what she was saying was true of a
great many articles seen in the newspapers, there might
be some truth in the theme of this article in relation to
her own life. How much of her enjoyment of shopping
had been because she had no outlet for other more semi-
nal urges?

To change the subject, she said, 'Tell me more about
your mother's collection of silver objects...and about
her.'

Although Reid's expression didn't change, she knew
intuitively that she had touched on an area of his life
which was off limits or had been until now. But surely
there should be no Keep Out areas between husband and
wife?

'Granny H asked me what flowers I was giving you.
When I said violets, she reminded me about the silver

collection. It's been in a safe deposit box since my parents separated and my mother left it behind.'

Although she was getting strong vibes that it wasn't a subject he wanted to discuss, Fran said, 'Why did they part?'

He shrugged. 'They didn't get on. They were incompatible.'

'How old were you when it happened?'

'I was at school. It didn't have much impact. Children are very resilient.'

The wine came. Not a carafe of house plonk but a bottle in an ice bucket. The waiter showed Reid the label. He nodded. The waiter poured a little into his glass. Reid put the glass to his nose and nodded again. The waiter filled both their glasses with the golden liquid, replaced the bottle on the ice and went off to attend to other people.

Reid picked up his glass and smiled at her. 'To us.'

'To us,' she echoed. The wine was chilled to perfection, refreshingly cool on the tongue but not refrigerated to the point where its sweet fragrance was lost.

'This has to be one of life's best experiences...sitting in a French pavement café on a warm evening, drinking a decent Bordeaux and watching the world and his wife...with your own far more beautiful wife,' Reid added gallantly.

If he had been in love with her, Fran could have believed he meant it. But he wasn't and she wasn't. She was content with her looks and knew she was attractive. Beautiful, no. Except to a man who adored her, and it didn't seem likely Reid would ever do that. He wasn't the adoring type.

'The last time I was here I was entertained by one of the "royals" of the wine trade in this region,' said Reid. 'It was like going back to the beginning of the century. There were twenty people—family and overseas guests—sitting round a huge table, being waited on by

men in tailcoats and gloves. The wines were the finest
I'm ever likely to drink. At first it was all rather formal...but by the end of the evening considerably less
so.' He laughed, showing a flash of white teeth.

'How come you were there?' she asked.

'Oh...bank connections,' he said vaguely. 'By the
way, I have a couple of things to attend to tomorrow
morning that would be boring for you. I hope you won't
mind amusing yourself. There's plenty to see in
Bordeaux...including some excellent shops.' He leaned
forward to take a leather billfold from the back pocket
of his trousers. Handing her a credit card, he said, 'Use
that for the time being. As soon as we get home, I'll set
up an account for you.'

Although, in a way, it was considerate of him to provide her with the means to shop without touching her
own by now much depleted funds, it was also a discom-
fiting reminder that, like the girl in the opera he had
talked about, she was a bartered bride. He had already
fulfilled his side of the trade-off. Very soon, perhaps in
a couple of hours, it would be her turn.

While they were eating dinner at a corner table inside
the bistro, Fran said, 'That French château in the folder
you showed me...does it belong to you now?'

'I went to have a look at it, but it needed a lot of
renovations and I wasn't sure I wanted to take it on. It's
about an hour's drive from here. Would you like to look
round the place? It's still for sale, I believe. Do you have
a yen for a château?'

Fran shook her head. 'I've never thought seriously
about living anywhere. I always assumed that when I
married I'd live wherever my husband needed to be.'

Reid gave her a thoughtful glance. By now it was dark
outside. The tables were lit by candles inside glass storm
shades. The soft upward light from the still flame em-

phasised his strong features and the brilliance of his eyes.

Although the bistro was popular and all the other tables were full, there was a sense of intimacy about being the only two foreigners in a room full of French people, in a city far away from where they had started the day.

'That's an old-fashioned attitude,' he said. 'I didn't think there were any women left who went along with that idea.'

'I don't have my own career to worry about. If I did, I expect I'd feel differently. Men have had it all their way for a long time. You can't blame women with interesting jobs for wanting to hang onto them.'

'I don't. I come into contact with a lot of career women. Some of them I admire. But I wouldn't agree that men have had it all their own way. Women have had a struggle to make themselves heard in the working world, but at home they've always had a lot of authority…if they chose to use it. They're the ones who have the most influence on the next generation. They also have pillow power…again if they choose to use it. A woman who makes a man happy in bed has a huge influence on him. How many of them actually run the world from behind the scenes we have no way of knowing.'

Fran couldn't think of any appropriate comment. With her mind focused on their return to the hotel, she found it hard to make table-talk. Even though she had chosen the lightest dishes on the menu, and the food here was very good, her appetite was at zero.

If only it had been Julian on the other side of the table, the initiation ahead of her would have been a long-awaited joy. Also she was fairly certain that, like her, Julian had abstained from casual couplings.

Reid, even if he had been discriminating in his choice of previous bed-partners, was undoubtedly far more experienced. He would be expecting her to be an exciting mate, not an unpractised virgin. In theory she knew all about what he called pillow power. But knowing those things and putting them into practice with a man she had known such a short time...

What am I doing here? she thought wildly. I must have been mad to think I could go through with this.

At the same time a part of her mind was asking, *What are you panicking about? There must be literally millions of women who would jump at the chance to go to bed with this man. He's everything most women dream about.*

But he's not the one I've spent half my life dreaming about.

That one's off limits, so what are you going to do about it? Spend the rest of your life mooning over someone you can't have? Get real. You're a married woman. It's too late for second thoughts...and you're not facing some kind of torture. This is a rite of passage all women have to go through. He's not going to make a hash of it. Chances are you'll enjoy it.

'Coffee?'

Reid's question closed down the link with her other self, the one who only came through in times of stress or indecision.

'Er...yes, please.'

As she had noticed before, he had the innate ability to attract a waiter's attention merely by glancing towards one. Having ordered coffee for them both, he said, 'What's on your mind, Francesca? You were looking worried just now.'

'Was I? I can't imagine why.'

'I can,' Reid said dryly.

'What do you mean?'

As casually as if he were discussing the weather, he said, 'Going to bed with someone new is always stressful for people who don't do it on a regular basis.'

Unnerved by his insight into her thought processes,

she found herself saying, '*You* don't look at all stressed. Do you do it on a regular basis?'

'Not in the sense you're talking about. I've had relationships. At my age it would be strange if I hadn't. If they'd been important, I wouldn't be here. Nor would you. Let's forget our separate pasts and concentrate on sharing the future.'

With the coffee came dark and caramelly Remy Martin cognac.

'To help you sleep,' said Reid, with a glint of amusement in his eyes.

It troubled her that he assumed she was equally free of emotional baggage. But there was no point in explaining. As he said, the past was the past. All that mattered was how to get along together from now on.

The walk back to the hotel took about fifteen minutes, including one or two pauses to look in the windows of shops.

'Should be a fine day tomorrow,' said Reid, looking up at the clear starlight sky.

To Fran, tomorrow seemed like the other side of one of those apparently bottomless chasms she had seen mountaineers crossing on rickety-looking ladders. But they knew what they were doing. She didn't. She was like a novice climber on an expedition with someone far more experienced who had no idea he had a tyro in tow.

There wasn't much traffic about now in the exclusive district where the hotel was located, but Reid still took her hand before they crossed the road. She hoped he wouldn't feel her having a bad case of the shakes. They were internal at the moment and she prayed that she could control them and not let him guess that she would have given her soul to be anywhere else but here.

In the lobby, Reid released her hand. He collected their key at the desk and they walked to the open lift and stepped inside.

Take a few deep breaths, said the voice of her alter

ego. *Remember the last time he kissed you. You were turned on then...it will be the same this time. Relax!*

But the calm voice of reason lived in an ivory tower at the back of her mind, removed from her heart and her senses which were causing her present panic.

The lift reached their floor. They stepped out and walked along the deserted corridor in silence, passing elegant console tables supporting lavish displays of flowers. One or two doors had expensive shoes outside them. This was not the sort of hotel where guests cleaned their own shoes, using a revolving brush machine at the end of the corridor. Fran wished it was less opulent. The de luxe ambience didn't intimidate her, but she might have felt more relaxed in a cosy rural *auberge*.

Reid fitted the key in the lock, opened the door of their suite and waited for her to precede him.

CHAPTER SEVEN

FRAN crossed the sitting room to look out through the tall French windows opening onto a balcony. Unbuttoning her jacket, she gazed at the view for a minute, then turned to see what Reid was doing.

He had also taken off his coat and dropped it onto a chair. Now he was coming towards her, moving at an unhurried but purposeful pace which told her, before he reached her, what he intended to do.

She inhaled a steadying breath, but this time the trick didn't work. As he reached her and put his arms round her, pent-up emotions welled up, finding relief in tears.

It was the most shaming moment of her life. She couldn't believe she was going to pieces like this, but her feelings were out of control. There was nothing she could do to stop the tears or the shuddering sobs that overwhelmed her.

Through it all Reid kept his arms lightly round her, gently stroking her back as if she were a distressed child. Presently he pushed a large linen handkerchief into her shaking hands.

His voice quiet and calm, he said, 'It's all right, Franny. Don't worry: it's just reaction to strain. What you need is some rest.'

His use of the pet name used by her family was unexpected. Mopping her eyes, she said in a choked voice, 'I'm sorry…I don't make a habit of this.'

'I'm sure you don't. These are exceptional circumstances. Look, I'm going to watch the news on CNN or NBC…whichever they're hooked up to. You go and brush your teeth and hop into bed. After eight hours' sleep, you'll feel a different person.'

'But—'

'No buts…just do as I say, there's a good girl.' He might have been addressing someone ten years her junior. He gave her a kindly push in the direction of the bedroom. 'Goodnight. Sleep well.'

Exhausted, grateful for his forbearance, she did as he told her.

When she woke up, the curtains were open. Last night they had been closed by the maid who had turned down both sides of the king-size bed.

For a moment or two Fran lay still, re-orienting herself after hours of dreamless oblivion. She was lying on her side, facing a pair of French windows which shared the balcony with those in the sitting room. Outside the sun was rising on the fine day Reid had forecast.

Reid! The thought of him was like an alarm bell going off in her mind. Where was he?

Cautiously, slowly, she edged onto her back, turning her head even further. Reid was asleep on the other side of the wide bed. He appeared to be naked. The bed-clothes were covering his lower back, but the upper part was exposed. As she had noticed yesterday, his skin had the sheen of brown silk. This morning his thick dark hair, usually brushed back from his forehead and as smooth as a blackbird's plumage, had been ruffled by his movements during the night. Behind his visible ear and along his neck it was forming little duck's tails.

Fran had always been a tactile person, attracted by textures ranging from bark to velvet. Now she was aware of an impulse to reach out and run her hand over the broad back, to touch the hair at his nape.

Instead she lay still, thinking about last night and how kind he had been, showing no hint of anger or frustration when, instead of fulfilling her side of their bargain, she had behaved like a hysterical idiot.

The memory of her breakdown made her bite her lip with annoyance. It was so unlike her to cry. She had never been a hysterical kind of person. She had always been strong…in control…

But Reid had been right: a long sleep had restored her. If not precisely eager, she felt equal to facing the day. What time was it? When would he wake up?

The answer to the first question was on her wrist. Usually she took her watch off before removing her make-up. Last night she had left it on, too zonked by emotion to bother with the normal bedtime routines. She had brushed her teeth, undressed, put on a nightdress and fallen into bed.

It was now a quarter to seven, the time she usually woke up. She would have expected Reid also to be an early riser. But what time had he come to bed? Maybe not until late, or rather early this morning.

As she was wondering whether it would be a good idea to make up for her behaviour last night by waking him with a kiss, there were signs that he was waking up anyway. The long body stirred and stretched. Then he rolled onto his back and started to open his eyes.

Just as she was expecting him to notice her and say hello or good morning, he shut his eyes tight and groaned.

For a moment she thought he must be ill. Could there have been something wrong with one of the oysters he'd had as a starter?

'Are you feeling sick?' she asked anxiously, hoping the hotel had a doctor on call. Food poisoning from shellfish could be serious.

It seemed he had forgotten she was there. Peering at her through half-closed eyes, he said, 'Not sick…just a bloody awful headache. My own fault. Too much brandy last night.' Wincing, he heaved himself up on his elbows, his eyes open now and not friendly.

'There's nothing like half a bottle of the hard stuff for sedating an over-active libido,' he told her sarcastically, before throwing back the bedclothes and swinging himself off the bed, smothering a curse as the movement aggravated his hangover.

It was Fran's first sight in real life of a totally naked male body and she only had a brief glimpse before he disappeared into the bathroom. What struck her was that even if the brandy had effectively doused his mating urges last night, the effect had worn off this morning. Walking from the bed to the bathroom, he had looked the personification of virility, at least from the neck down.

She wondered whether to get up, put on a robe and step out on the balcony for some fresh air. She hadn't noticed it earlier, but there was a strong smell of brandy hanging in the air and, with two people sleeping here and the window closed, the atmosphere must be stuffy.

She hopped out of bed, opened both the French windows and, in the act of picking up the slightly more opaque robe that went with the filmy nightgown, paused.

After a shower, he might feel sufficiently restored to want to consummate their union. If she was out of bed he might see it as another rebuff.

She climbed back into bed and lay listening to the muted sound of the shower. How much was it going to hurt? Hopefully not very much, if he was an experienced and considerate lover. Sleep had restored her resilience. This morning she was back to normal. Equal to anything. Perhaps even slightly looking forward to ceasing to be a virgin and becoming, at long last, a fully fledged woman.

It was almost half an hour before Reid reappeared, the dark stubble gone from his jaw, a towel wrapped round his lean hips and his masculinity no longer noticeable, except in the sense that every line of his body from his shoulders to his strong but shapely ankles was indisputably male.

'All yours,' he said, barely glancing at her as he made for the chest of drawers where he had stowed his things.

Fran slipped out of bed, conscious that her Italian nightdress was designed to entice not conceal. But Reid didn't turn his head as she circled the bed.

Perhaps, despite his refreshed appearance, he still had a pounding headache, or perhaps he was giving her more time to come to terms with her conjugal obligations.

As before when they had shared a bathroom, he had left it immaculate. When Fran was small, the Turners had lived in a house with only one bathroom. There had always been stubble in the basin and splashes on the mirror after her father had shaved. Despite being outnumbered by women, he had always left the seat up. Reid, married for less than twenty-four hours and not at his best, had remembered to put it down. His thoughtfulness touched her.

He had left the bedroom when she returned to it. When she joined him in the sitting room, he was reading a French newspaper he must have ordered when he registered.

'Let's have breakfast downstairs, shall we?'

She wondered why he preferred to eat in public rather than up here *à deux*. 'I have some paracetamol with me if you'd like some?' she offered.

'I never use them, thanks. Coffee will clear what's left of my headache. Sorry if I snarled at you earlier.'

'It was my fault you felt like snarling. I'm sorry about last night. You were right: some sleep has restored me. I guess even a quiet wedding is quite a stressful occasion.' She smiled at him. 'Can we make a fresh start?'

'Of course.' But his smile was guarded, as if it would take a good deal more than an apology to wipe out the memory of last night's fiasco.

The hotel catered to an international clientele with breakfasts to suit all tastes. They both chose the French breakfast, although it was Fran who ate most of the freshly baked, hot croissants. Reid drank a lot of orange juice and coffee.

Until he started making suggestions as to how she might spend the morning, she had forgotten they weren't going to be together. He didn't even tell her where he was going or why, only where they would meet for lunch and at what time.

In any other circumstances, the prospect of spending a few hours in a historic foreign city would have had Fran flying to the main information centre to review the possibilities. But as Reid had already listed the main attractions, that wasn't necessary. She had only to choose the most appealing of the options.

They parted in the ground-floor lobby. He didn't kiss her goodbye. Not even a peck on the cheek.

She was left feeling snubbed and forlorn. His plan to go off on his own had been made *before* what happened last night. Even if they had made love and everything had been hunky-dory between them, he would still have deserted her.

Not really in the mood for either sightseeing or shopping, she spent some time exploring the old part of the city where a lot of the buildings dated back to the fifteenth century. She was early arriving at their rendezvous where there was a sunny terrace with tables shaded by sunbrellas.

She ordered a lemon drink and settled down to write cheerful postcards to Gran, her mother and Shelley. She was addressing the second when her ballpoint died on her. She gave an exasperated sigh.

'May I lend you mine?' someone said, in strongly accented English. It was the man at the next table. She had noticed when he sat down that he was young and good-looking but after the briefest glance she had looked away.

'That's very kind of you.' She accepted his offer and finished what she was doing, aware that he was watching her and wondering if he intended to chat her up. If so, he was wasting his time...although, come to think of it, it might be no bad thing for Reid to realise that other men found her attractive.

She gave the pen back. 'Thank you.'

'My pleasure. Are you on holiday?'

'Yes. Are you from Bordeaux?'

At first the conversation followed the usual lines. He introduced himself as Gilbert and told her he was an architectural draughtsman with aspirations to be a full-time painter.

'Bordeaux has produced many artists...Odilon Redon...Rosa Bonheur. She was the first woman ever to receive the Legion of Honour. The government gave her official permission to dress as a man.'

'Why did she want to do that?' Fran asked.

'She specialised in painting animals and cross-dressing made it easier for her to sit about at fairs and markets, painting the cattle and horses. She lived in the nineteenth century when women had much less freedom. Not like now when they can go anywhere...do anything.'

He had been admiring Fran's hair, and telling her how much he would enjoy painting her, when she saw Reid arriving but pretended not to.

Her husband didn't look pleased at finding a stranger leaning towards her, his hand on the back of her chair. As he came within earshot, Gilbert was asking her if she would be willing to pose for him.

Reid answered for her. 'Certainly not,' he said coldly. 'My wife's time is fully occupied.'

Gilbert jumped to his feet, looking almost laughably embarrassed. Fran would have felt more contrite about keeping her left hand out of his line of sight since deciding to make use of him had she not suspected him of exaggerating his artistic talents. Surely a bona fide artist would have been sufficiently observant to notice her rings while she was writing the postcards? He might even not be a draughtsman. The whole story could be a line.

'Excuse me...I didn't realise...' Pulverised by the laser-like glare fixed on him by the tall Englishman, Gilbert withdrew in confusion.

'I should have thought by now you would have perfected the technique of fending off passes,' Reid remarked curtly, as he sat down.

'It hadn't got to that stage, or anywhere near it.' Fran explained about the ballpoint.

A waiter arrived with the drinks list and two menus. Reid ordered a litre bottle of water. Glancing at Fran's tall glass, he said, freezingly polite, 'Another soft drink for you?'

'A glass of white wine for me, please.' Because he was on the wagon, she didn't see why she should be.

Judging by the angry tic in his cheek, she might need a little Dutch courage.

Last night at the bistro, Reid had spent a long time studying the menu before making up his mind. Now he gave it only a cursory inspection before deciding on an entrecôte with a salad.

'I'd like a little more time, please.' Fran smiled sweetly at the waiter.

'Certainly, *madame*.'

Knowing Reid was irritated, perhaps because he was impatient to say some more cutting things to her, Fran took her time before deciding on fillets of sea bass with artichokes.

'And to begin, *madame*?' the waiter enquired.

'Nothing, thank you...but perhaps a pudding later.'

'Some wine with the entrecôte, *monsieur*?'

'No, thank you.' Even with the waiter, Reid's tone was markedly lacking in his usual affability.

As soon as they were alone, he said in a low cold voice, 'Let me make something clear. Our marriage may be unusual in some respects. It isn't and never will be an "open" relationship. You belong to me now. If anyone else sends out signals, I expect you to make it clear you're already spoken for.'

'In that case it would make sense not to leave me hanging about while you're busy with more important things,' she said angrily. 'A wife isn't a possession...at least not in our part of the world. She's supposed to be an equal partner. If you're going to be jealous if I even speak to other men, we might as well separate now. I couldn't stand it.'

This statement was followed by an interval of fraught silence because the waiter had come back with a basket of bread and was making adjustments to the table settings.

'If you didn't want to be left on your own, why didn't you say so?' Reid asked, a few minutes later.

'Because it was obvious that, whatever it was you had to do, you preferred to do it alone.'

'Rubbish! I was going to the outskirts...to one of the commercial zones. It's not an interesting area. I thought you'd prefer the centre.'

'What were you doing there?'

'Buying some equipment the French are particularly good at.'

He didn't elaborate. She could tell he was still in a rage and not without justification. She *had* encouraged poor Gilbert to believe she was here on her own. But if Reid couldn't see that it was outrageously selfish to leave a bride by herself on the first day of a honeymoon, he deserved to be taught a lesson.

Their food came. In any other circumstances Fran would have savoured every mouthful. Today she ate it mechanically, torn between outrage at Reid's macho outlook and regret that they were at loggerheads.

Trying to consider the situation dispassionately, she felt it boiled down to the fact that Bordeaux wasn't a suitable place for a honeymoon. Maybe, when a couple were in love, anywhere would be heaven. But even then a romantic and peaceful setting had to be better than a huge crowded city.

When the time came, she decided against a pudding, knowing she wouldn't enjoy it in an atmosphere of repressed disharmony. They were giving a good imitation of the kind of couple who had long since exhausted their conversational resources and had nothing left to say to each other.

They had coffee and Reid paid the bill. Outside the restaurant, he flagged a taxi.

As it sped them back to the hotel, she had the feeling that, as soon as they reached the suite, he intended to make punitive love to her...with or without her compliance.

She cast a surreptitious glance at his averted face. He was staring out of the window. All she could see were the angular lines of his cheekbone and jaw. He had said she belonged to him. Was he capable of taking her, regardless of her wishes? What was he really like at the core of his being? Was there savagery there, even cruelty, under the civilised surface? Last night he had been kind. But perhaps he was losing patience with her.

In the lift going up to their floor, Fran's insides were full of butterflies. But this wasn't the same kind of panic she had felt when they came back last night. Now there was an element of excitement mixed in with the apprehensiveness.

Reid unlocked their door. Even though he was annoyed, he didn't stride in ahead of her but stood back for her to precede him.

'Thank you,' she said, matching his politeness.

'How long will it take you to pack?'

Taken aback, she swung round and gaped at him. 'We're going back to London?'

'Don't be silly. We're moving on. You didn't imagine we'd be spending the whole trip in Bordeaux, did you?'

'What else was I supposed to think?'

He made for the bedroom, saying over his shoulder, 'You wanted a magical mystery tour. We're on our way to one of the most beautiful parts of Europe...the mountain valleys of the Basses Pyrénées. Bordeaux was merely a stopover to avoid driving on last night.'

'How are we getting there?'

'I've rented a car. You can share the driving if you like. Have you done any driving on the right?'

'A little bit, in the States.'

As Fran began to pack, she felt relieved that the rift between them had been bridged. But also, if she were honest, she was a little disappointed that their quarrel hadn't been resolved in the manner she had half expected.

Until they had been to bed together, until she was over *that* hurdle, there was bound to be tension between them. Sex was, after all, what honeymoons were about, even though, for most of her contemporaries, the sexual side of their honeymoons was a continuation rather than a beginning as it would be for her.

An hour after leaving the hotel, they had left Bordeaux behind and were heading south towards the western end of the mountains which ran from the Mediterranean to the Atlantic, forming a natural frontier between France to the north of them and Spain to the south of them.

Using a well-known computer program, Reid had charted their route from Bordeaux to the small French country town which was to be their next night stop. He had passed this to Fran as an aid to her job as navigator.

But as the journey progressed, it seemed to her that he knew the way by heart.

'Do you know the Pyrenees well?' she asked.

'Parts of them, yes. They're addictive. The weather's not too reliable, but it never is in the mountains, unless you go much further south.'

Although much of their route was on fast roads through flat country, by the afternoon's end they were in the foothills of the mountains whose distant peaks were still gleamed with snow.

The roads became narrower, the terrain more alpine. When Reid drove into the car park of a small hotel called La Terrasse, it could be seen at a glance that it was a very different establishment from the one in Bordeaux. Several old countrymen and a younger one in the distinctive blue overalls of the French working man broke off a gossip in the bar when Fran walked in ahead of Reid who immediately greeted them and received a polite chorus of 'M'sieur...dame' in response.

They were given a key and found their own way upstairs to a room on the first floor which was in darkness until she switched on the light. It was about the size of their bathroom in Bordeaux. A low divan bed occupied most of the space. The television, high up on the wall, looked like a oversize security camera beamed on the bed.

'Not too pokey for you, I hope?' said Reid, putting down the cases.

She didn't mind it for herself, but was a little surprised that he found it acceptable. Like the suite in Bordeaux, this room also had French windows but on a smaller scale and inward-opening because there were louvred doors outside them. She pushed these open and stepped out onto a timber-built balcony roofed by the projecting eaves typical of buildings in regions where, in winter, heavy snow fell.

'Oh...what a fabulous view!'

Beyond the head of the valley they had been following rose majestic peaks, their snowfields glistening in the soft evening sunlight. In the middle distance high pastures sloped down to tracts of dense woodland.

'Nice, isn't it?' said Reid.

She glanced at him, seeing on his face an expression new to her. She was trying to think of a word to describe it when there was a tap on the door and he went to open it.

The large middle-aged woman who had given them the key came in with a tray bearing a wine cooler and two glasses.

'Did you order this in advance?' Fran asked, when they were alone again and he was opening the champagne.

He nodded. 'I'm told by the women in my family that, at the end of a long drive, a hot bath and a glass of champagne are the best possible pick-me-up. I'll have a quick shower first and then you can laze in the bath for as long as you like. The dining room opens at eight.'

'You've stayed here before?'

'Yes...but not in this room and I was on my own, taking a few days' break.' Having filled the glasses, he said, 'Let's take them outside, shall we? But first...' He reached out to take her hand and draw her towards him. 'Shall we kiss and make up?'

Fran put her hands on his chest. Instinct told her that here in this unpretentious hostelry in its lovely setting, things were going to go better.

'I'm sorry about today, Reid. I did flirt a bit with that Frenchman, but only to pay you out for—as I thought—neglecting me. I believed we were in Bordeaux for you to do banking things.'

'You must think I'm extraordinarily passionate about banking to give it priority even on my honeymoon.'

By almost perceptible degrees his arms were tightening round her, pressing her closer against him.

'Most people with interesting careers are passionate about them. I understand that. It was just that I felt, in the circumstances, you should be concentrating on me.'

'I intend to concentrate on you. From now on you'll have my undivided attention.' He bent his head and kissed her, but only lightly.

Even so it was enough to make her pulses start to race. She was disappointed when he let her go and handed her one of the glasses.

The balcony had two director's chairs propped against the inside wall. Reid set his glass on the rail of the balustrade while he unfolded them.

'Tomorrow I'll take you up there,' he said, his eyes on the pastures, after they had sat down. 'It's great walking country. At this time of year we shall have it almost to ourselves.'

'Are there still bears in these mountains?'

'A few, in the more remote areas. Also a lot of wild boar. I've occasionally smelt them and heard them, but they keep out of sight. There's plenty of interesting bird life and it's a botanist's paradise.'

He drank his champagne rather quickly and went in to have his shower. Listening to the water running, Fran wondered if, while she was in the tub, he would lie on the bed, wrapped in a towel, waiting for her to join him, intending to make love to her before they went down to dinner.

The sound of bleating made her stand up and lean over the balcony. Coming along a side street below was a large flock of sheep, a man leading them and a dog bringing up the rear. As he passed the hotel, the shepherd looked up, acknowledging her with a nod. She wondered if he had ever been away from this valley or had spent his whole life here.

She thought back to how Reid had looked on first seeing the view. He had stood with his hands on the rail and his eyes on the mountains. It had seemed to her that he had undergone some subtle transformation, becoming more relaxed and approachable. Or had she only imagined it?

As he had that morning, he came out of the bathroom with a towel wrapped round him.

'I'm afraid it's rather steamy in there. There's no window, only an extractor fan. Let me refill your glass.'

He had already run a bath for her, she discovered. Lying in the warm water to which she had added some of her own bath oil, she sipped her second glass of champagne and wondered if he had drawn the glass curtains to make the room more private and folded back the bedclothes.

Although he said, 'Take your time. There's no hurry,' she felt she ought not to keep him waiting too long. After all they had been married for almost thirty-six hours and so far, for various reasons, it hadn't been much of a honeymoon for a man who, by any standards, had been extremely patient.

Fran was just about to stand up and start drying herself when there was a tap on the door.

'It isn't locked. You can come in.'

The door didn't open. Speaking through it, he said, 'I'm going down to order a picnic for tomorrow. When you're ready, we'll have a stroll round. OK?'

'OK,' she echoed, half relieved, half disappointed that the moment of truth had been put off till later.

When she went downstairs the locals had gone from the bar and Reid was having a drink with two people with backpacks on the floor by their chairs.

He and the man both rose as Fran joined them. Reid said, 'This is my wife. We're Reid and Francesca Kennard.'

'We're Ben and Jenny Lewis. How d'you do, Mrs Kennard.' The man extended his hand and his wife shook hands with Reid.

Both in their middle fifties and looking extremely fit, the Lewises, as she soon gathered, were midway through a walking holiday. They had been lucky with the weather, spending every day following parts of a complex network of sheep and cattle tracks.

They always spent their holidays walking. Ben was an experienced climber but his wife had a poor head for heights so they didn't climb together.

At first Fran thought they were at La Terrasse for a drink, but it turned out that they were staying there. When they went up to their room, Reid and Fran had their stroll.

The town had an ancient clock tower, a World War One cenotaph with a sculpture of a wounded soldier, and buildings of every period since the fourteenth century. More or less parallel with the through road was a small gurgling river spanned by a granite bridge. Nearby, in a small meadow under the spreading branches of a sweet chestnut tree, hens scratched in the grass.

'That's a nice sight,' said Reid. 'Hens living out of doors as nature intended.'

Fran had been thinking the same thing.

As they moved on, he took her hand. 'Do you like it here?'

'Very much. It's a lovely place.'

'I thought we'd stay here for two nights and then move on somewhere else. If you like, later on, we could cross the frontier and try a few nights in Spain.'

'Do you speak Spanish?'

'Enough to get by.'

He continued to hold her hand all the way back to the hotel, only letting it go in order to open the door for her. As they entered, Mr and Mrs Lewis were coming down the stairs.

'We're both starving,' said Jenny. 'Eight hours in the open air works up a massive appetite. As we seem to be the only people staying here, shall we join forces for dinner?'

'By all means,' Reid agreed. 'If there are only the four of us, it does seem a bit antisocial to sit at separate tables.'

The meal with the Lewises was the first one Fran had enjoyed since they arrived in France. It turned out that, like Ben, Reid was an experienced and enthusiastic rock climber. While they talked about that, Jenny explained her job, giving technical support to people who had bought computers from one of the best-known manufacturers in the UK.

Purely as a pastime, Fran had bought a PC and taught herself to use it. So she was able to ask intelligent questions and was much amused by Jenny's tales of some of the crankier people who used the hotline.

'How long have you two been married?' Reid asked, during the cheese course.

It was Jenny who answered him. 'Thirty-five years in September. It seems to have gone in a flash, doesn't it, Ben?'

Smiling, her husband agreed. 'We married too young...our families thought. But so far so good,' he said—with a teasing sideways glance at his wife.

'Unfortunately our children haven't been as lucky,' said Jenny. 'Our son is divorced and our daughter is living with someone. There's so much of that these days. It's a nice change to meet a young couple who are a Mr and Mrs. To me, all these so-called partnerships aren't the same as a real commitment. I think they're a cop-out.'

Clearly she was assuming that Reid and Fran had been married some time and had no idea they were newly-weds.

'What's the secret of your success, do you think?' Reid asked.

'Friendship,' said Ben. 'The difference between a

marriage that lasts and one that doesn't is friendship.
That's what it really boils down to.'

As soon as they had finished eating, the Lewises said
goodnight and retired to their room. By now there were
some late arrivals in the dining room, but none of them
was English.

'You seemed to find Jenny good company. You were
laughing a lot,' said Reid, while they were drinking coffee.

Fran repeated one of the anecdotes. It made him laugh
too.

Then, as the smile faded, something else came into
his eyes. He said quietly, 'Would you like some more
fresh air...or shall we go up?'

Fran held his gaze. 'Let's go up.'

A new smile made little curls at the corners of his
mouth. 'There's still some coffee in the pot.'

'I don't want any more. Do you?'

Her right hand was on the table, toying with the stem
of her empty wine glass. Reid took it and lifted it to his
lips, brushing a kiss across her knuckles. Even more
softly, he said, 'No...I want you.'

They put their checked cotton napkins on the table
and rose. As they did so, there was a commotion in the
bar-cum-reception area. A policeman and another man
had come in and were talking to the *patron's* wife whose
response conveyed agitation.

As Reid and Fran left the dining room, the policeman
gave him an assessing look, then spoke to him in French.

The conversation that followed was too rapid-fire for
Fran to follow any of it.

CHAPTER EIGHT

HALF an hour later she was back at the table, sharing a fresh pot of coffee with Jenny. Both their husbands were out with the mountain rescue team which, being short-handed that night, had had to seek volunteers in the local hotels.

All the two women knew about the accident was that it had happened some time that afternoon. Two foreign girls had been climbing together. One had fallen and been badly injured. The other, returning to their hotel for help, had mistaken the way and got lost.

'It's lucky Ben and Reid were here,' said Jenny. 'If the injured girl is stuck on a ledge halfway up a rock face, they'll need a full team to get her down.' She shuddered. 'It makes me feel bad just thinking about it. I can't bear to watch Ben climbing. I wish I could share it with him, but I don't feel safe on the top of a step-ladder. Do you have a good head for heights?'

'I really don't know,' said Fran. 'I've never done any climbing.'

She was wondering how long the rescue would take. A long time, by the sound of it. It might be the early hours of tomorrow morning before Reid came back.

'You may enjoy it. What does Reid do for a living?'

'He's a banker.'

'Really?' Jenny seemed amazed. 'He looks such a fit, outdoorsy kind of man. I can't imagine him stuck in an office all day. Does he enjoy it?'

'It's a family tradition. His father, grandfather and great-grandfather were bankers.'

'Oh I see...so there was a lot of pressure on him.'

Jenny's tone was commiserative. 'It was a bit like that for Ben. At the time he left school climbing wasn't a career option. His father was a dentist so Ben followed in his footsteps, even though it never really fulfilled him. He's longing for retirement so that he can begin to enjoy himself full-time. I feel that, in that respect, he's wasted his life,' she ended, with a sigh.

'What does your son do?' asked Fran.

They had been chatting for an hour when Jenny said, 'I think we should go to bed. There's no point in sitting up.'

Alone in the double divan where, but for the unforeseen emergency, she would now be in a deep postcoital sleep, Fran lay awake for a long time. It had been a strange sort of day, beginning badly and ending inconclusively.

But there had been some moments to remember with pleasure. Reid holding her hand while they strolled and kissing it at the table, his face neither angry nor cold, as it had been earlier, but warmed by desire.

She had responded...then. The wine they had drunk, the conversation at dinner, the encouraging success of the Lewises' marriage had all combined to make her feel hopeful that she and Reid could shape the strangeness of their relationship into something good and enduring.

But would that optimism still be in place in the morning?

She woke up with a start to find Reid standing at the foot of the bed. She had fallen asleep with the light on. Struggling into a sitting position, she was about to ask him what had happened when he put a finger to his lips, tapped his wristwatch and held up four fingers.

Then he came and sat down close to her, saying in a low voice, 'Panic over. The girl is on her way to hospital. Her arm is broken but she's going to be OK. I'm sorry I woke you.'

'It doesn't matter,' she whispered. 'You must be exhausted. Would you like a cup of tea?' The room was equipped with a kettle, crockery and a choice of tea, coffee or chocolate.

'I'd rather have a kiss.'

Before she was properly awake, she was in his arms, being kissed with startling enthusiasm considering that, twenty-one hours ago, he had woken up with a hangover and had just spent half the night assisting a rescue in the middle of nowhere.

Roused from a confusing dream, with her mind still in subconscious mode, Fran was functioning by instinct, and the messages coming from instinct were to go with the flow.

His face was cold from the night air and he smelt different from usual. But his mouth was warm and she liked being held in strong arms. Her lips softened and parted under the pressure of his.

It would have been nice to continue the kiss indefinitely, but suddenly he put an end to it. 'I'm filthy,' he murmured in her ear. 'I can't come to bed like this. I'll have a quick shower.' He moved to the end of the bed and bent to unlace his boots.

Before he and Ben set out, she had discovered that the boots, and a pair of light ones for her, had been in his luggage all the time. He had found out her size from her mother. His other climbing equipment—the stuff he had bought in Bordeaux—had been in the boot of the car he'd rented.

The boots off, he stood up and shed the rest of his clothing, except for his undershorts. Then he disappeared and moments later she heard the shower running. Would it disturb the people in the next room? she wondered. With so few people in the hotel, perhaps that room was empty.

Waiting for him to come back, she identified the unfamiliar aroma as sweat from strenuous exertion. She pushed back the bedclothes, swung her feet to the floor and picked up the coral-coloured sweatshirt he had stripped off. Only the faintest trace of his body scent lingered on the garment but she found it curiously exciting.

The noise of the shower stopped. There was a pause. Then she heard him brushing his teeth.

I need to brush mine, she thought.

She was standing near the bathroom door when he came out, vigorously towelling his head, a hand towel worn like a loincloth.

'I shan't be long.' She slipped inside, closed the door, and splashed her face with cold water before reaching for her toothbrush.

The bedroom light was out and Reid was standing by the window when she rejoined him. Fran extinguished the bathroom light. She had discovered earlier that, with the shutters open, the bedroom was never in total darkness because, although they overlooked a side street, there was a powerful street lamp where it joined the main road.

It would take a little while for her eyes to adjust to the dimness after the brightness in the bathroom. But Reid's eyes had adjusted. He came to where she was standing and took her face between his hands.

'It was hard to concentrate on what I was doing...hard not to think about you.' He resumed the interrupted kiss, his hands gliding down the sides of her neck, along her shoulders and then down her back to her waist where they pulled her closer against him.

For a moment or two Fran was passive, her hands trapped between them against the solid wall of his chest, her fingertips feeling, for the first time, the burnished texture of his bare skin.

The sensation of being held close by someone much bigger and stronger, against whom, if he chose, she was powerless, was strangely exciting, like swimming in a rough sea.

Knowing the time for restraint was over, that she owed it to him to be generous with her responses, she ran her hands up his chest to the strong column of his neck and then slid her forearms behind it, pressing herself against him in implicit abandonment.

She heard his sharp intake of breath and felt his broad chest expand against the softness of her breasts. Then his hands moved down from her waist, slowly caressing her flanks until, catching her by surprise, he took hold of the skirt of her nightdress and pulled it slowly upwards.

Fran stepped back to allow him to draw it over her head and toss it aside. All her shyness seemed to have vanished. A second later she was being swung off her feet and held like a bride being carried over a threshold. Seconds after that he was lowering her onto the bed, pausing only to dispose of his own covering before following her down. He had, she realised, already thrown back the top bedclothes, leaving only the smooth undersheet. Hours earlier she had disposed of the sausage-shaped bolster, replacing it with the two large square pillows found in the top of the wardrobe.

In the dim silvery light, the bed looked like a low table spread with a white damask cloth, or perhaps a white marble altar prepared for some ancient ritual.

As Reid loomed over her, a dark silhouette with only the shape of his head and the outlines of his shoulders discernible, she felt like a virgin being sacrificed to a god. But such a magnificent god that she welcomed her immolation.

'You're so beautiful...' His voice was a husky whisper. Leaning on one elbow, he placed the flat of his other hand on the space between her breasts and her navel. Immediately every sensitive part of her body felt as if it were switching on, like a computer booting up before the opening screen of a mind-blowing program.

Slowly, his hand moved upwards and outwards to glide up the swell of her breast and pause on the summit, his palm still open, the heel of his hand moving lightly in a caress of such exquisite subtlety that it made her gasp with pleasure.

Like a hawk dropping out of the sky, his mouth seized her parted lips in a kiss that set up a network of delicious sensations. For the first time she felt the coaxing warmth of his tongue and her own instinctive response. She was conscious of being surprised that it all felt so easy and natural, as if they had done this before in other times, other lives, and were rediscovering each other. She knew now it was right to have waited, that only with this one man...

The thought came into her mind, only to evaporate as she felt his hand coasting downwards to explore the curl of her navel and all the territory south of it, the flat plane between her hipbones, the thicket of dark red curls and beyond, like two long smooth dunes, the curving lines of her thighs.

Gently, he moved them apart, tracing patterns of delight on the sensitive inner skin, making her breathing quicken, her heart beat in rapid thumps as his fingertips moved tantalisingly close to the place where she wanted to feel them, only to move away.

Suddenly he rolled her over, kissing a path down her spine while he ran a possessive hand over her behind and, finally, sank his teeth into the soft flesh in a series of playful bites, making Fran bury her face in the feather pillow to stifle small animal sounds she couldn't repress.

He turned her onto her back, starting to kiss her breasts. It was almost twenty-four hours since he had shaved. His chin and cheeks felt rough, but she found that exciting. Everything about him thrilled her. She plunged her hands in his hair, her body arching as his marauding mouth sent streaks of ecstatic feeling zinging along her nerves.

Dimly, her own emotions already out of control, she was aware that he hadn't reached that point. Somehow, by sheer force of will, he was still in charge of them both, his own feelings firmly leashed while he drove her mad with longing.

At last she felt his hand where she wanted it to be, searching for and finding the key to the ultimate pleasure. There was nothing tentative in his touch. He knew exactly what she needed to drive her over the edge. Almost at once, she was there, free-falling off the edge of the world in a white-out of feeling she had never achieved on her own.

Limp, exhausted, drained, she came slowly back to her senses. 'Oh, Reid...why? Why not together?'

'Together comes later.' Even speaking in an undertone, his voice had a hungry rasp that sent a small frisson of trepidation through her. What was he expecting of her? Something more than she could give? Was she going to disappoint him?

He began to make love to her again, kissing her mouth, softly stroking her body. Amazingly it wasn't long before she began to feel flickers of renewed arousal irradiating from the core of her body out to her fingertips and toes. This time the magic worked faster. This time, driven by impatience to relieve that amazing sensation, she felt for the hand caressing her and led it to its destination.

She felt Reid tense and knew by his smothered exclamation that her inviting gesture had stretched his control almost to breaking point. But this time he didn't touch her where he had before. His fingers explored beyond that, searching and parting the delicate folds of tissue as if he were touching the petals of an exotic flower.

She could feel his heart pounding now. His skin burned against her hand. As a car went past on the main road, its headlights shone into the room like the moving beam of a lighthouse. For a brief shining instant the face above hers was illuminated. She saw the glitter in his eyes, the fierce mask of controlled desire.

Then, without meaning to, he hurt her.

Her teeth set, she drew in a sharp breath.

Immediately the pain stopped. 'Darling...what is it?'

He had never called her 'darling' in private before.

'It's nothing...nothing.'

'Don't be silly. I hurt you. Why are you tensing?'

She had known he was going to find out. How could it be otherwise? But she'd thought it would only be afterwards that he would realise she had been a virgin. It hadn't occurred to her that he might find out earlier, that she would have to tell him.

'I'm not. It's just...I haven't done this before.'

She had wondered how he would react when he found out and assumed that, apart from being surprised, he wouldn't have any strong feelings on the subject. Her father's generation still seemed to have a problem accepting that aspect of equality. Younger men took it for granted that women had all the same rights to freedom that they did.

'Are you saying that you've never made love?'

'Yes.'

What happened next was totally unexpected. His arm arched above her head and he snapped on one of the reading lights.

'Why the hell didn't you tell me?' he demanded, his voice no longer an amorous murmur but an angry growl.

Taken aback by his abrupt change of mood, Fran said, 'I didn't think it mattered.'

That made him spring off the bed, snatching up the towel and wrapping it rapidly round him.

Fran had nothing to cover herself with, nor did she want to. After his tender exploration of her body, why should she want to hide it from him? But as lying down while he was standing made him look even taller and more forbidding, she hitched herself into a sitting position.

'You didn't think it mattered!'' Reid repeated her statement in a tone of savage sarcasm.

'Why should it? What's the difference?'

'The difference is that you lied to me,' he snarled at her.

'I did *not* lie! The subject never came up.'

'You lied by default...knowing damn well I thought you had some experience.'

'Well, I haven't,' she snapped back, 'and some men would think it a plus. I don't understand your problem with it.'

For a fraction of a second he looked at her rather blankly. But perhaps she had only imagined it. An instant later, he said coldly, 'I don't like being taken for a ride. If—'

He stopped short at the sound of someone rapping on the wall behind the bedhead, reminding them both what time it was and that for the last few minutes they had been speaking in raised voices.

'We'll talk in the morning,' Reid said, resuming an undertone.

But instead of getting into bed and lying down with his back to her, as she expected, he began to get dressed.

'Where are you going?' she asked, in a baffled whisper.

'Out...it will be light soon. Go back to sleep,' he instructed.

'You have to be joking!' she hissed.

Reid gave her a dark brooding glance then continued dressing, his every movement expressive of silent fury.

When he had gone, Fran got out of bed to replace the bedclothes and put on her nightdress. He had left her in a state of physical and mental turmoil. The only thing to be done about it for the time being was to take a leaf out of Gran's book and make herself a calming cup of tea.

By the time it was fully light, she had made and drunk three cups of tea and was feeling a lot more composed and equal to handling her husband when he decided to come back.

The possibility that he might not come back, or only to pick up his things and inform her the marriage was over, had crossed her mind briefly. But after a moment's thought, she had dismissed it. Maybe non-consummation was grounds for divorce when it was the result of some physical problem or the bride's refusal to participate. But if the bride was willing and it was the groom who had a hang-up, then it would be up to her to have the marriage annulled.

Which is *not* what I want, thought Fran.

Although it was still very early and everyone else in the building, except possibly a cleaner, would be asleep, she had a bath and dressed in jeans and white tee shirt, one of a stack she had bought on a shopping spree in Hong Kong. They had been her best bargain, being intended for Chinese workmen which made them a nice snug fit.

By the time she had done her face, although the valley was still in the shadow of the mountains to the east, the sun had reached the high pastures. The cloudless sky overhead signalled it was going to be a lovely day...at least weather-wise.

Wondering where Reid had gone, Fran decided that, rather than hanging about metaphorically biting her nails until he chose to return, she would go out herself.

The *patron's* wife was already bustling about downstairs. They said *'Bonjour, madame'* to each other. Fran wondered if she was being over-sensitive in feeling the Frenchwoman was watching her with a beady eye as she went out of the door.

Would the people in the room next door complain to Madame about being disturbed? she wondered, following the direction they had taken yesterday evening. Well, that was the least of her worries. Making peace with Reid was the only thing that really mattered.

It concerned her that, having been out most of the night, he should still be up and about, instead of catching up on his sleep in a comfortable bed.

Whatever their temporary differences, as Gran had told her, from now on her primary function was to make life easy and, if possible, happy for him.

A few days before the, to her mind, soulless performance at the register office, she had reread the marriage service in the Book of Common Prayer presented to her mother on the day of her confirmation. Its contents included the Form of Solemnization of Matrimony in the old-fashioned wording in use then, phrases that read like poetry.

Wilt thou have this man to thy wedded husband...Wilt thou obey him, and serve him, love, honour, and keep him in sickness and in health; and, forsaking all other, keep thee only unto him, so long as ye both shall live?

The promise she would have made, had they been married in church in Mum's day, or Gran's day, would have been, *I Francesca take thee Reid to my wedded husband, to have and to hold from this day forward, for better for worse, for richer for poorer, in sickness and in health, to love, cherish, and to obey, till death us do part...and thereto I give thee my troth.*

Fran had read those vows for the first time when she was fifteen, dreaming of marriage to Julian. They were still the words she associated with marriage; the promises which, in her heart, she had made in the register office.

Even the word 'obey' didn't bother her. Her feeling was that if you were sharing your life with a man and the chips were down—the ship sinking, the aircraft on fire, a madman with an axe breaking down the front door—you expected your guy to be capable of handling the situation, giving orders which you, and anyone else who happened to be around, would be only too pleased to obey.

By the time she reached the little stone bridge over the river, the sun was catching the ripples and making them shine. The air smelt of green vegetation with a faint whiff of the farmyard.

Further along the bank on the village side, there was a wooden bench where, last evening, two elderly men in Basque-style berets had been having a chat.

Now it was occupied by a younger man, his long frame bent at the knees to fit between the cast-iron armrests at either end.

As Fran hurried towards him, she guessed he had sat down to watch the river and only later decided to catch some shut-eye. The gilet he had been wearing when he stormed out of the bedroom was now folded under his head and his arms were folded across his midriff.

Like most people, sleeping he looked much younger. But there was the trace of a frown between his dark eyebrows, as if he had still been angry when sleep overtook him.

She wondered how long it would be before he woke up. She didn't intend to disturb him, only to hang about until he woke up naturally. It didn't seem likely he'd sleep for long on a couple of planks.

There was nowhere for her to sit except on the dew-damp grass. Her sneakers making no sound, she walked up and down the path, rehearsing what she would say when he woke up.

Then a local appeared, carrying a bucket. She could see he was going to speak to her so she put her finger to her lips as Reid had when she woke up. The man seemed to understand the gesture. She hoped that, de-

spite looking a bit simple-minded, he would pass Reid
without making a noise.

Instead, after peering at the recumbent foreigner so
closely that she thought his heavy breathing might wake
Reid, he straightened, saying something in an incompre-
hensible local accent before crackling with raucous
laughter at his own, probably lewd, comment. Reid
stirred and looked up at him before saying something
that sounded like a French expletive.

The man looked aggrieved but didn't argue. As he
shambled away, Reid sat up, rubbing his hands over his
eyes, then stretching his arms above his head and flexing
his shoulders.

'Good morning,' Fran said quietly, from the other end
of the bench.

He didn't look pleased to see her. She hadn't expected
he would.

'What are you doing out here?'

'Looking for you. What else? I was worried about
you.'

He glanced at his watch, then rubbed a hand over his
jaw. 'I'll need to shave before breakfast.'

'If you have any sense you'll go back to bed until
lunchtime. I can amuse myself.'

'I may do that.' He stood up.

'Reid…I'm sorry about last night.' She lifted her chin
to look him squarely in the eyes. 'I didn't mean to mis-
lead you, but I still can't see what difference it makes.'

'You can't, hmm? Then I'll spell it out for you. There
are cultures where sexual inexperience is a plus. It used
to be that way in ours. Not any more. I thought I was
marrying a woman who knew what it was all about…not
someone who had no idea.'

'You make it sound something incredibly difficult that
takes years to learn. That's ridiculous. Any fool can do
it.'

'They can and they do,' he said grimly. 'But if they

were getting it right there would be fewer divorces and most of the shrinks and sexologists would be out of business. I didn't expect to have a tyro on my hands.'

Determined not to be routed, she said, 'I should have thought that was preferable to having a man-eater on your hands. At least I shan't be able to make any odious comparisons if your expertise as a lover falls short of perfection.'

She expected a crushing rejoinder. To her surprise, an unwilling smile softened the set of his mouth.

After a moment, he said, 'You have a point there, I suppose.'

For the rest of the way he was silent and Fran thought it best to hold her tongue. Back at La Terrasse he went upstairs to shave and she flipped through some French magazines from a basket of visitors' discards at the foot of the stairs.

Presently he came down and they went in to breakfast, soon to be joined by Jenny who said she could never sleep past her usual getting-up time but Ben was still dead to the world. She expected him to stay that way for several hours more.

'Why don't you two take the car and have a look round the shops in Oloron-Sainte-Marie?' Reid suggested. 'By the time you get back, Ben and I will be back on form.'

'Good idea,' Jenny agreed. 'Are you happy with that, Francesca?'

When they came back at lunchtime, they found the men in the garden at the back of La Terrasse, drinking lager and talking about climbing.

Ben suggested spending the afternoon as a foursome, but Jenny, who had found out the Kennards were on their honeymoon said, 'These two are newly-weds. I'm sure they'd like the rest of the day on their own.'

Rather to Fran's surprise, Reid didn't contradict her.

They had a light lunch together and then the others went off and he and she were alone.

'Shall we go for a walk?' he suggested. 'It would be a good idea to try out your boots.'

In their room they both changed into shorts. When she had put on the boots, Reid laced them for her. As he half knelt at her feet, one knee on the floor, she was intensely conscious of how the day had begun.

It would be so easy to put her arms round his neck and, when he looked up, to lean forward and kiss him. It felt like the right thing to do, but it might be the wrong thing. Perhaps it was wiser to wait and leave the initiative to him.

They walked for about an hour before he suggested a rest stop. Before they left the hotel he had made a flask of tea and, on the way out of town, had bought a large bar of chocolate.

Fran sat on the grass, her back against a felled tree trunk, and watched him opening his rucksack. She wondered what he was thinking. Even though the place where they were had beautiful views on all sides, she couldn't relax and enjoy them. Her mind was focused on her relationship with him. But perhaps, being a man, with a mind that worked in a different way, he had closed off the compartment reserved for emotion and sex, and was thinking only about their tea break.

'How do your feet feel?' he asked.

'Fine. The boots still feel a little strange, but perfectly comfortable.'

'You'll soon get used to them.' He handed her a plastic cup and four squares of chocolate.

'Thanks.' She bit into the chocolate, watching a herd of cows grazing in a meadow further down the hillside. As the chocolate melted on her tongue, she remembered his kisses, an even more sensuous experience.

She wished he would kiss her again but a quick glance in his direction showed him looking stern and remote.

'I've been thinking it over,' he said. 'For someone of your age never to have had a lover, there has to be a powerful reason. There are two possibilities.' He turned his head to look at her. 'One is that you're a convert to the cult of celibacy...'

He paused, obviously expecting her to confirm or deny it. Would he believe her if she said yes? Somehow she didn't think so and anyway she wasn't comfortable lying. She shook her head.

'Or you've been saving yourself for one particular man.'

'Something like that,' she admitted. 'But it's over...it's finished.'

'Why?'

'He married someone else.'

'Do you still love him?'

She hesitated. It wasn't a simple yes or no answer. You didn't stop loving people because they were unattainable. At the same time there was no point in breaking your heart over someone you could never have. Life was too short, too precious, to be wasted on vain regrets.

'Well?' Reid's tone was impatient.

'I'm getting over it,' she said.

'You should have told me,' he said curtly. 'You're guilty of false pretences.'

Her green eyes sparkled indignantly. 'I am not! Love wasn't part of the deal...on either side. For all I know, you might have suggested this marriage because you were in the same boat...in love with someone you could never have.'

'In that case I should have told you...been straight with you.'

'And I should have told you that I didn't want to know...that your past is your business...not mine. Anyway what's done is done.'

Her simmering temper boiled over. 'Really your only beef is that I'm not experienced. Well, tough! You should have read the small print more carefully. Your investigator did tell you I'd been "extremely discreet". That should have given you a clue that my qualifications didn't include a long list of torrid affairs and the expertise of a call-girl.'

'Calm down…have some more chocolate.' Reid tossed the bar towards her.

Fran caught it and threw it back, aiming to hit his chest. To her annoyance he fielded it, her childish retaliation only serving to amuse him.

She was tired, she realised. Not as tired as he had been earlier. But she'd still lost several hours' sleep, besides being put through the wringer emotionally.

Draining her plastic cup, she scrambled up. 'If you don't mind I'm going back. I'd like some time on my own.' She put the cup by the flask.

'Are you sure you can find the way?'

She knew it was his intention to return to the village by a loop and they were about halfway along it.

'Don't worry: I have an excellent sense of direction. I'll see you back at the ranch.'

Reid watched her walk away, her back very straight and the set of her shoulders indicative of barely contained rage.

Her shorts showed off her long legs. On some girls the combination of good legs with walking boots and rolled-down thick socks could be sexier than sheer tights and high heels.

He had once had a brief affair with a French climber met on a difficult rock climb in Spain's Picos de Europa mountains. They had had a great deal in common, but she had been on home leave from a job in Africa so there had been no future in it.

Now he was saddled with a wife whose passionate mouth and self-confident walk had misled him into ex-

pecting an enthusiastic bed-partner, but who turned out
to be carrying a torch for someone else.

It showed she had a lot of character and that, in the
long run, was good. A woman with a mind of her own
was preferable to a dim-wit who followed the herd.

But someone burdened with the emotional baggage of
an unhappy romance was more than he had bargained
for. Nor had he ever expected to have to deflower a
virgin, for God's sake.

Reid re-packed his rucksack and stood up. She might
have a good sense of direction as she claimed, but forest
tracks looked different in reverse and, in her present
mood, she might easily take a wrong turning. He would
have preferred to go on according to plan, but felt he
should follow her down and make sure she didn't get
lost.

Setting a leisurely pace so as not to overtake her, he
was torn between annoyance at her stupid deception and
unwilling sympathy for her.

At the beginning he had thought she was marrying
him to maintain her easy way of life. Now he suspected
her main motive had been to spare her mother from the
consequences of the bankruptcy. For different reasons,
he had felt the same way about his father. But the solution for him hadn't been as drastic as the one she had
grabbed.

At least we have that in common, he thought som-
brely. We are both in a trap.

Back at the hotel, Fran took off the boots and lay down,
hoping it would be a while before Reid reappeared. As
a relaxation exercise she closed her eyes and forced herself not to think about anything but an imaginary dot in
the centre of a blank page.

The trick worked. When she woke up, it was an hour
and a half later and she felt refreshed and more equal to

coping with the evening ahead. She wondered where Reid was.

Perhaps he was having a drink with the Lewises.

She showered and shampooed her hair, blew it dry and used a styling mousse to comb it into shape. Then she put on a minimum of make-up and went to the wardrobe. She was taking out the simple shirt dress she had worn the night before when Reid walked in.

For a second or two his eyes scanned her slim body only partially concealed by a lacy bra and matching briefs. Then he turned away and poured himself a glass of spring water from the litre bottle he had brought up the night before.

'I've been thinking things over,' he said.

Fran buttoned the dress and watched his reflection in the mirror behind the dressing-table-cum-desk.

'Have you? I've been asleep,' she said, sounding calmer than she felt. 'What conclusions did you come to?'

He didn't turn round but looked at her through the mirror, as if he wanted to depersonalise what he was going to say. She had an ominous feeling she wasn't going to like it.

CHAPTER NINE

'I THINK we should treat the rest of this trip as a holiday rather than a honeymoon. Obviously we don't know as much about each other as we thought we did. We need to fill in those gaps before we can...come to terms.'

Before Fran could make any comment, Reid went on, 'The Lewises are leaving tomorrow. I thought we'd have dinner with them and then move on to a place they've recommended. It's not far. If we pack now and leave about nine, we can be there before ten. I've checked that they have a room free and paid the bill here.'

She wondered why he wanted to leave tonight instead of waiting till tomorrow. The charge for the room was on a printed notice pinned to the back of the door. It was far less than the cost of staying in an equivalent hotel in Britain and clearly the waste of money was a matter of indifference to Reid, as it would have once been to her.

But a bankruptcy in the family had made her see everything differently. Even though she was now the wife of a rich man, she would never again be recklessly extravagant.

At dinner, no one would have guessed from Reid's manner that, since the previous evening, his relationship with his bride had been through a crisis. Secure in their own long and stable relationship, Ben and Jenny remained unaware of the unresolved problem hanging over their new acquaintances.

The two men split the bill and exchanged addresses and Jenny gave Fran a warm hug. 'I hope we see you again. Enjoy yourselves...well, of course you will,' she said, laughing, as if it were a law of life that a honey-moon must be blissful.

Driving deeper into the mountains, along twisty roads where, in places, melt-water streams poured down the hillside and disappeared into culverts under the road, should have been a joyous adventure. But Fran couldn't rid herself of the feeling that Reid had some underlying purpose in this hurried departure from La Terrasse.

'What's the next place called?' she asked.

'Les Trois Sommets, *le sommet* meaning the mountain peak.' Reid changed down to swing the car neatly round another hairpin. It was clear he was used to driving on serpentine mountain roads.

There was a party taking place in the dining room at Les Trois Sommets. The *patron* was with the merry-makers, but saw Reid and Fran arriving and came to welcome them, insisting on taking one of the suitcases and showing them the way to their room.

The first thing Fran noticed, as he switched on the light, was that it had twin beds.

When she woke up next morning, the other bed was empty and the bathroom door was open.

Reid was chatting to the *patron* when she went down-stairs.

'I'm sorry I overslept.' She had lain awake a long time, listening to his regular breathing from the other bed.

'It doesn't matter. Did you sleep well?'

'Yes, thank you. And you?'

'I always do,' he said briskly.

They might, she thought, have been two people on a group holiday. Their next topic would be what the weather was going to do.

On cue, Reid said, 'It's going to be another fine day so I've ordered a picnic lunch. Ben told me about a small lake…a good spot to have a picnic.'

They had the lake to themselves, an idyllic spot where they watched a kite hovering high ahead. 'They're quite rare in England now,' Reid said, handing over his field glasses for her to take a closer look.

For the rest of the week they spent long hours walking, evenings playing board games or cards—Reid could play bridge but didn't seem to mind that Fran could only play rummy—and slept in their separate beds. He made a point of getting up early and coming to bed after she'd finished in the bathroom.

They might, she thought, have been a financially pressed brother and sister economising by sharing a room. Except that there were times when her feelings about him were anything but sisterly.

One night, over dinner, she said to him, 'Jenny was talking to me about the pressure Ben felt to follow his father into dentistry. Did you ever feel you'd like to break the tradition?'

It seemed to her that he gave her a reflective look before he said, 'Yes, many times, but it would have upset my father. He'd been very broken up when my mother left him. By the time I was eighteen he was fighting cancer. I couldn't add to his burdens by rejecting the career he'd mapped out for me.'

'What would you have chosen to do?'

Reid gave a sardonic laugh. 'I wanted to go into a partnership with a guy I knew who was setting up a wilderness travel company. It seemed a risky undertaking at the beginning, but he's done very well.'

'After your father died, couldn't you have given up banking then?'

'By then I had missed the boat,' he said with a shrug.

'Why? You're still only in your thirties. You're terrifically fit. People switch careers all the time...often it's forced on them.'

'If I'd switched careers,' he said dryly, 'I shouldn't

have been able to pick up the pieces from your father's disaster...nor would you have agreed to marry me.'

She flushed. 'That would have been no great loss. You might have married for love.'

'My father did that,' he said cynically. 'It didn't bring him much happiness.'

'Why did your mother leave him?'

'She was bored and unhappy. She ran away with a travel writer.'

'How old were you when she left?'

'Ten. But I was away at school so it didn't have a lot of impact. I always preferred my father.'

I wonder if that's true? she thought. Or was it the way he coped with being deserted by her? How could she have done that to him? How could any woman leave a child at such a vulnerable age? The anger she felt towards the unknown woman surprised her.

'Has she ever made contact with you?'

'She's tried. I'm not interested,' he said coldly. 'And I don't need an amateur psychologist probing my psyche, Francesca. I know women enjoy self-analysis and baring their souls to friends. Men don't.'

'Perhaps if they did they'd be less of a pain in the whatsit,' Fran retorted robustly.

That made him laugh. She found when she answered back he seemed to prefer it to when she was meek and mild.

He changed the subject. 'Would you like to move on, or are you happy to stay here another day?'

'Whatever you say. You're in charge.'

The next morning he taught her to abseil, using a rope and metal clips called karabiners to lower herself down a rock face. By lunchtime Fran had discovered that being suspended halfway down a small cliff didn't bother her. She could look down without feeling either giddy or panicky.

In the afternoon she watched him working his way up a much higher escarpment she would have thought was unclimbable. At first he went up it as easily as a steeple-jack on scaffolding. Then he came to a more difficult stretch.

Suddenly she couldn't bear to watch him. But when she rolled onto her tummy on the stretch of warm turf where he'd left her and tried to read a paperback, she found it impossible to concentrate. She *had* to sit up and watch Reid and the rest of the time he was on the face of the cliff was one of the most unpleasant ten minutes she could remember.

By the time he rejoined her, having found a way to walk down, she had pulled herself together, at least outwardly. The experience had reminded her of an incident in her childhood, a visit to a circus whose performers included a family of acrobats. The rest of the audience had enjoyed their feats on the trapezes and the high wire. Fran had felt increasingly queasy. While everyone else was applauding what the ringmaster described as death-defying stunts unequalled in the history of the circus, she had had to be hurried outside to be physically sick on the grass outside the big top. When Reid came striding towards her, a look of satisfaction on his face, his bare chest and shoulders slick with sweat from the exertion of the climb, she told herself that the knotted feeling inside her had been the same reaction she had felt as a child.

Some people got a thrill out of watching others take risks and a few people found it scary. Watching Reid had been worse than watching the acrobats because for him there had been no safety net.

'Do you often climb on your own?' she asked, as he dried himself on a small towel he kept in his pack.

'I have...up to now. It occurred to me, halfway up, that today had better be the last time. If I'd dropped off while I was up there, it wouldn't have been a nice experience for you…or for me, come to that,' he added humorously.

'How can you joke about it?' Fran hadn't intended to say anything about her reaction to the climb, but she couldn't help sounding irritated when he made light of the horrific risk he had taken.

Reid tilted a quizzical eyebrow at her. 'There are worse ways to go. It would have been over in seconds…and you look very fetching in black, I remember.'

'That's not funny!'

'I should have thought the prospect of being a rich widow might be rather pleasing.'

She glared at him. Without pausing to consider the wisdom of firing off the first retort that came into her head, she said angrily, 'I'm not even properly your wife yet. If you *had* fallen off that cliff, I wouldn't have touched a penny of your money. I'm only in this situation because of my mother. If I hadn't needed help for her, I'd have told you to go to hell.'

Reid dropped the towel on the grass and thrust his hands into the pockets of his shorts, a gesture suggesting that he might be restraining an impulse to place them round her neck and squeeze.

'You did,' he reminded her. 'But then you thought better of it.' His face an impenetrable mask, he went on, 'The arrangements made for your mother will remain in place whatever happens. Our marriage, as you point out, isn't fixed in stone…not yet. If you want to have it annulled…' He left the rest in the air.

She took a deep breath. 'I didn't say that…I don't. I—I just resent the implication that I'm a gold-digger, out for all I can get. It's not true.'

He bent to pick up his tee shirt, slipping it over his head before thrusting his arms through the sleeves and pulling it down over his washboard midriff.

'I know that, Francesca. If you had been, I wouldn't have married you. Let's start making tracks, shall we?'

The rest of the day followed the pattern of previous days. Earlier, after his pre-breakfast shower, Reid had shaved with an ordinary razor, but after his pre-dinner shower he used an electric razor to remove the slight shadow appearing round his mouth and along the hard outlines of his jaw. She heard it buzzing while she was having her bath. Usually by the time she had finished in the bathroom, he had dressed and gone downstairs to read a paper or magazine until she joined him for a drink.

This evening, not hearing the outer door close, she expected him still to be there when she returned to the bedroom. But he wasn't, and she felt a pang of disappointment. What had she been hoping? That he would be lying on the bed, waiting for her like the eager lover of her dreams?

While she was dressing she thought about what he had said to her earlier. Did *he* want the marriage annulled? Had he realised that his plan had gone wrong...had been a mistake from the outset?

'I think tomorrow we might cross the frontier and take a look at the Spanish side of the mountains,' said Reid, during dinner. 'I'll ring the *parador* tonight...make sure they've got a room for us.'

Fran spooned up the last of her pineapple *millefeuille*. But instead of raising it to her lips, she met his eyes across the table. 'Do you know the Spanish for twin beds?'

'*Camas gemelas.*'

'What a marvellous vocabulary you must have. I can't believe you've ever needed those words before.'

'That's right,' he said blandly.

She had told him, and meant it, that his past was not her business. Why then did it hurt her to think of him holidaying in Spain with someone else?

'I'll go and make the call now. You can order the coffee, can't you?'

Fran nodded. Watching him walk away, his body as lithe as a leopard's, she realised that every day, every hour, his attraction for her grew more powerful. This afternoon, if something had gone wrong, all that remained of that potent masculinity would be in a French morgue and she would be facing the rest of her life without ever knowing what it was like to belong to him.

When the waiter came to take away their pudding plates, instead of asking for coffee, Fran managed to tell him they wouldn't be having it tonight. Would he please tell her husband that she was waiting for him in their room?

'*D'accord, madame.*' His smile added a subtext to his polite reply: he wouldn't mind being in her husband's shoes.

Fran needed the boost to morale his unspoken admiration gave her. Was she doing the right thing?

In their room, she went to the bathroom and quickly brushed her teeth. She was undressing when she heard Reid enter. Seconds later he tapped on the bathroom door. 'Fran…are you all right?'

'I'm fine. I'll be out in a minute.'

She wrapped a towel around her, sarong-fashion, and remembered to take off her earrings and her engagement ring, the only jewellery she was wearing.

As the hotel was a haven for walkers, climbers, botanists and bird-watchers, the dress code was informal. Even in the evening shorts were seen in the dining room. Tonight Reid was wearing a clean pair of pale cream chinos and a dark blue cotton shirt.

When she opened the bathroom door, he had unfastened the buttons to show a strip of tanned chest but the shirt was still tucked in his trousers.

He stood with his hands on his hips, the thumbs to the back, male-style. 'It's early to turn in, isn't it?'

She closed the door behind her and moved to where he was standing between the beds and the window. 'You can have enough rummy. Tonight I'd rather…make love.' She moved even closer and slipped a hand inside his open shirt, pressing her palm against the warm brown skin over his breastbone.

He clapped a hand over her hand. She could feel the tension in him.

'Are you sure about that, Francesca? As things stand you can still back out.'

'So can you. Do you want that?'

For a moment longer he gave her a brooding stare and she couldn't tell if he would say yes or no. Then he said in a low husky voice, 'I want you,' and, taking hold of the towel, he whipped it away before crushing her naked body in his arms and kissing her with a passion that made her doubts seem ridiculous.

When she woke up in the morning, in his bed, he wasn't with her. But the other bed hadn't been used so, despite the limited space, he must have stayed with her until he got up.

In a way she was glad to have some time to herself, to adjust to being, at long last, fully a woman, seeing life from a new perspective, *knowing* instead of wondering. For some people finding out was a disappointment, a let-down. Not for her. It had gone beyond her expectations, far beyond. The momentary spasm of pain had been nothing compared to the pleasure before and after it. Reid was a terrific lover.

She stretched and jumped out of bed. Today they were going to Spain, and tonight, unless the hotel was crowded, unlikely at this season, they'd be sleeping in a double bed with masses of room to…

She smiled at her lecherous thoughts and hurried to run a bath.

Her buoyant mood was slightly deflated when she ran

downstairs and found him reading a paper, not looking like a man for whom the desert had bloomed. But of course for him it hadn't been a new experience, she reminded herself. He had done it before...many times, with partners who matched his own skill.

Smiling, she said, '*Bonjour, m'sieur.*'

He rose, putting aside the paper. '*Bonjour, madame.*'

There were no other guests about yet. Would he have kissed her if, just at that moment, the hotelier hadn't emerged from the rear of the premises?

After saying good morning, the Frenchman said, 'You are leaving today. I hope you've enjoyed your visit and want to return another time.'

'I'm sure we shall.'

As the two men went on chatting, Fran wondered if they would come back. Perhaps, although he had needed a woman, what had happened last night had been a flawed satisfaction for Reid. She had often thought that, except for a very unimaginative man, an act of love which involved inflicting pain, even unavoidable pain, must be a strange experience. To have to do that without love must be even stranger. No wonder he had been angry at finding she was a virgin.

She came out of her thoughts to find the *patron* had gone and Reid was passing his hand in front of her face.

'Oh...sorry.' After a pause, she added, 'I'm in a bit of a daze this morning.'

'Is that good or bad?'

'Good...very good.' On impulse, she curled a hand round his wrist and rubbed her cheek against his upper arm. 'Thank you for making it so good for me.'

He was smiling as he said, 'That's actually the object of the exercise. Didn't you know?'

'That might be the theory. I don't think it always works in real life. You said the other day...that if people were getting it right there wouldn't be all these divorces.'

There were other guests coming downstairs. Reid said, 'Let's concentrate on breakfast. We can talk about sex when we get to our next destination,' he added, with a teasing look that sent an anticipatory thrill of excitement through her.

By ten, they were on their way. Half an hour later they were above the treeline in a region where the air was cooler and the road was lined with tall poles banded with colour to mark the depth of snow during the winter months. It was wild, barren country inhabited only by small groups of wild goats.

Where once there had been a frontier post, now there were only deserted police and customs buildings. They crossed from France into Spain without any formalities.

The *parador* was an ancient castle converted by the Spanish government into a luxurious hotel. Fran wondered if Reid would remember that he had asked for twin beds.

He did and, without any sign of embarrassment, informed the desk clerk that they would now prefer a *cama matrimonio*. 'And I'd like a bottle of *cava* sent up immediately, please.'

'Certainly, *señor*.' The clerk spoke excellent English. What he thought about people who wanted twin beds one day and a double the next, they would never know.

Their room was a return to the luxury of Bordeaux but in the Spanish taste. While they were starting to unpack, the *cava* arrived with a complimentary basket of fruit. The waiter opened the bottle and poured the pale golden wine into two crystal flutes. Some notes changed hands and he bowed himself out.

Reid picked up the glasses and came to where Fran was standing beside her suitcase.

'As a concession to foreigners, the restaurants in most *paradores* open about half past one, although Spanish people eat later,' he told her. 'If we're going to keep

Spanish hours while we're here, we have a couple of hours to spare.'

'We could go for a stroll,' she suggested.

'We could…or I could give you another tutorial. Yesterday I taught you to abseil. Today I could give you a lesson in something more fundamental.' He touched his glass to hers before drinking some of the *cava*. 'How to make love to a man.'

Fran's insides did double somersaults. She gulped down some wine. It tasted the same as champagne.

'All right,' she said breathlessly.

Reid took her by her free hand and led her to the huge bed with its brocaded cover. He whipped this back with a single strong flick of the wrist. Then he sat down on the edge.

'You can start by undressing for me…slowly.'

For a second she froze with shyness. Then she thought, OK…why not? I've got the underwear for it.

Draining her glass, she said, 'Wait just one minute. If I'm going to let my hair down, I need some more of this…' She fetched the bottle in its bucket of crushed ice and put it on the nearest night-table. 'Some more for you?'

'Uh-uh.' Reid shook his head, a slight smile curling his mouth as he watched her refill her glass and take another swallow before setting it down.

'Now…' Fran's eyes sparkled with a mischievous determination to give him at least as much as he expected of her and possibly a good deal more.

Although all her outer clothes were simple separates, with just one ravishing slither of almond-pink dévoré velvet in case they went dancing one evening, all her underpinnings were seductive bits of lace and satin from an Italian firm specialising in luxurious lingerie.

So far Reid had seen only the briefest glimpses of it. Now he would get the full impact.

To start, she unfastened her hair, held back and up by

a couple of tortoiseshell spring clips. Shaking it out, teasing it into wild disarray with her fingers, she gave him the sultry smile she had practised in front of mirrors when she was a teenager but never actually used in real life. If strip-tease was what he wanted, it was what he was going to get—with bells and whistles!

Keeping his eyes on her, Reid stretched a long arm to put his glass on the night-table. Fran began to unbutton her white cotton sleeveless top, slipping it off her shoulders with the exaggerated shrugs she had seen strippers do in movies. Her bra was the colour of lemons and designed to maximise her curves. She took a slow deep breath, her hands fooling around with her hair, to make him wait for her next move.

Reid watched but showed no reaction other than the amused lift at the corner of his mouth.

Determined to make him pant, she unbuckled her belt and pulled it slowly through the loop of her jeans. They had a buttoned fly which, when they were new, had taken for ever to undo. Now the denim had softened and they unfastened easily, but she did it slowly, pausing between each button to inch the jeans down her hips.

Reid's expression remained annoyingly impassive. She suspected that was deliberate. But he certainly didn't look bored. She had his full attention.

'Oops!' She faked a naughty-me giggle and clutched the front of her briefs to prevent them going down with the jeans as she wriggled them over her bottom and let them fall to her ankles. She had already heeled off her deck shoes. Now she stepped out of the jeans and kicked them out of the way.

It seemed a good moment to knock back some more of the *cava* before going on to the next stage. By now she could feel the bubbles beginning to fizz through her veins.

'I think I might have missed my vocation,' she purred,

sliding one strap of her bra off the end of her shoulder, then doing the same with the other.

'Perhaps you have,' Reid agreed, the husky timbre of his voice confirming that the stoic face was a mask.

Fran put her hands behind her to unfasten her bra. 'Are you ready for this?' she teased, moving a step closer to him.

His hands were resting on his thighs, just above his knees, his body inclined slightly forward. She noticed his fingers tightening and saw the tic at his jaw before he managed to relax it.

For the first time she felt a stirring of sensual power. Perhaps she could do to him what he'd done to her last night…reduce him to mindless ecstasy.

She released the clip, peeling the bra away from her breasts and freeing her left arm from the thin strand of ribbon. It only needed a rippling movement of her torso to send the flimsy garment fluttering to the floor.

Naked except for her briefs, she said softly, 'If we're going to play games, I think you're overdressed.'

As she stepped between his legs and started to undo his shirt, she glanced down at him and saw that he was gripping his thighs to stop himself touching her.

It was a heady sensation, knowing she had it in her to drive this controlled and commanding man wild. And this was only the beginning…

The hard lithe shape of his body made it easy to pull his shirt free of his trousers and push it off his suntanned shoulders. While Reid put his hands behind him to finish taking it off, she slid down onto her knees to flip the tongue of his belt out of the matt brass buckle. He lay back to make it easier for her to pull down the zip. But first Fran took off his dark brown loafers.

'You have much nicer feet than most men,' she said, caressing one of them, knowing it wasn't his feet he wanted her hands on.

Reid has his fingers laced at the back of his head. He

was watching her from a quarter way through a sit-up, a position he made look as effortless as lying on a pile of pillows.

She remembered from last night the feel of that hard strong body against her own softer flesh and the wonderful sense of togetherness when it was over. She wanted those feelings again, but not yet.

To help her take off his chinos, Reid relaxed his shoulders and lifted his heels onto the edge of the bed to lever his backside off it. Some loose change and a bunch of keys slipped out of his pocket but they both ignored them.

Fran pulled his trousers clear of his hips, pretended to lose her balance and fell forward onto his stomach. 'Sorry.' She removed herself with a leisurely press-up, her expression demure.

'You can do it again if you like.' He gave her a wolfish grin, his narrowed eyes gleaming.

'Legs straight, please.' She made herself sound like a staff nurse dealing with a difficult patient.

Reid obediently straightened his legs for her to pull his trousers off. Aware that his eyes were caressing her, she deliberately took her time placing the chinos' hems together and hanging them neatly over the back of a chair.

Turning back to the bed, she found that Reid had used the brief interval to whip off his undershorts and move fully onto the bed. He beckoned her to join him. 'I'm beginning to think there's not very much I can teach you,' he said, as she climbed on beside him.

'I'm sure you can. What ought my next move to be?' She sat back on her heels and gave him a wide-eyed smile, fixing her eyes on his face, pretending not to notice that he was already powerfully aroused.

'Let's see what your instinct comes up with.' He was breathing faster than usual, the grey eyes she had thought cold now like slits in the wall of a furnace.

'Well…' With a series of rapid movements she disposed of her tiny briefs and arranged herself close beside him. 'My instinct says this might be nice.'

Ten minutes later she had the satisfaction of seeing Reid sprawled on his back, his head flung back, his eyes closed, his white teeth bared in a rictus of almost unbearable pleasure.

It was an empowering moment that filled her with a strange tenderness. Somehow it made him more human and made her feel better about the nature of their relationship.

Aware of an unfamiliar kind of happiness, she bent to repeat the caress which had made him groan with enjoyment. But as her hair, falling forward, brushed softly across his body, he put out his hands to stop her.

In a single convulsive moment, he reared up and pushed her backwards, fitting their bodies together, bringing his mouth down on hers.

Even the late-lunching Spaniards were already eating when the head waiter greeted the Kennards and led them to a table for two.

While Reid talked to him in Spanish, Fran turned the pages of the menu till she came to an English version. Having woken out of a short but deep sleep and dressed in a rush, she didn't feel ready to make even simple decisions.

'Shall I choose for both of us?' Reid asked.

'Would you? That would be lovely.'

Amazed that he could snap back to normal so quickly, she sat in a pleasant daze while he made the decisions.

When they were alone, he said, 'When I was a small boy I used to enjoy cartoons about a cat who was always getting banged on the head and seeing stars. You look the way he used to look when someone had thumped him with a saucepan.'

'I'm not surprised,' she said, smiling, not minding his teasing.

'Perhaps it would have been better to have something sent up by Room Service. Or perhaps not,' he added dryly, with a look that added a subtext she had no trouble reading.

Leaning across the table, he put out his hand palm upwards. When Fran gave him hers, he squeezed her fingers. 'You're fantastic. I've heard of women having a natural gift for it. Obviously you're one of them. I can't believe my luck.'

'I could say the same about you,' Fran answered lightly.

She was glad they had found one level where they were in total rapport. But was it enough to build a good marriage on?

CHAPTER TEN

THEY spent the last night of their honeymoon at a small château-hotel on a beautiful stretch of the Garonne, a place of pastoral tranquillity less than an hour's drive from Bordeaux.

Fran had lost count of the times they had made love. She had started the trip as an uneasy novice. Now she felt she had more than caught up with her experienced girlfriends. Judging by things they had let drop, in the terms of physical pleasure she was way ahead of them.

But although in Reid's arms she had found a whole new dimension to life, she wasn't as happy as she ought to be.

South-west France was enjoying an early heatwave. They had dinner outside on the terrace. Most of the other visitors were well-heeled Americans and Fran was glad she'd decided to wear the dévoré velvet slip-dress.

When she joined Reid downstairs, he said, 'You look ravishing, darling,' and kissed her hands.

But later, during dinner, he said something that worried her. 'You were saying the other day that your schooling was a waste of time. Why not do something about that…sign on with the Open University and get yourself a degree in a subject that interests you?' he suggested. 'Most of the women I meet, socially and professionally, spend hours a week toning their bodies but they don't do a lot about exercising their minds.'

'Surely their jobs do that?'

'Not necessarily. Careers give people a focus, but often it's a narrow one.'

He changed the subject and she sensed that for him

the end of their honeymoon and the resumption of normal life was something he didn't want to think about until they landed in London.

An hour later, in a bedroom furnished with heirlooms and faded *toile de Jouy* curtains framing the open windows, they made love by moonlight. It was good for them both, but afterwards, instead of falling asleep in his arms until Reid woke her by lifting his body from hers, Fran stayed awake, thinking.

Had his remark at dinner indicated that although he enjoyed her in bed, he found her less entertaining outside the bedroom?

On the flight home she made up her mind to prove herself, but not necessarily in the way he suggested. To work for a degree without a specific purpose seemed to her pointless. She wanted a more practical project.

In the weeks after their return, their life formed a pattern of weekends looking for a house in the country, returning to London on Monday morning and leaving on Friday afternoon. Many of the houses they looked at would have suited Fran but Reid's requirements were more exacting. Nothing they saw satisfied him. She began to feel nothing would.

In London, often she had Lady K breathing down her neck. When her grandson was out of the way, that formidable personage had no compunction about invading his young wife's privacy in their rooms at the top of the house.

They had been married for almost two months when they went to a large dinner party given by a society hostess whose mission in life, according to a magazine profile, was to bring together the best younger brains in the country.

Fran wore black, with the emerald beads and an emerald shawl trimmed with a long silk fringe. Reid looked distinguished in black tie but was not in a party mood.

Fran's schooling had made her at ease in all social circles, but those in which she had moved before her marriage had been mainly made up of frivolous pleasure-seekers. She didn't expect to know any of the people at this party. It was a surprise and a shock to recognise two of the faces in a crowd of strangers.

When their hostess introduced them to Julian and Alice, he said, 'Franny and I are friends from way back,' and leaned forward to kiss her on both cheeks.

In the taxi taking them home at the end of the evening, Reid said, 'You and Julian Wallace seemed to have plenty to talk about.'

Aware that he hadn't liked it when, after dinner, Julian had drawn her aside to speak to her privately, she said, 'We grew up together…almost like brother and sister. Julian thinks his father is fond of my mother. He feels they should get together. But he knows his father won't say anything without some encouragement from Mum. He asked me to suss out her feelings.'

'How do you feel about that?'

'It might be a good thing…better than Mum spending the rest of her life on her own.'

The taxi drew up at the house. Reid sprang out and offered his hand as he always did, but she felt that to-night it was an automatic gesture. He paid the fare, un-locked the front door with his key, and they crossed the hall and went up the staircase in silence.

In their bedroom, they undressed on opposite sides of the large room. Suddenly Reid said, 'It's obviously Wallace's wife who wears the trousers. He struck me as a wimp.'

'How can you possibly judge him on such a brief acquaintance?'

'How long does it take?' he said scathingly. 'The man may have a good brain, but that's no use without judg-ment.'

'He may have excellent judgment. How would you know?' Fran retorted defensively.

'He has lousy judgment,' said Reid. 'He could have had you. He chose her.'

Fran went white. 'I don't know what you're talking about.'

He came to her side of the room and took hold of her chin. 'Don't lie to me, Francesca. I needed to know who it was you were in love with. Your grandmother told me. Now let me tell you something. If it's at the back of your mind that encouraging your mother to shack up with her ex-chauffeur will give you a good excuse to see more of Wallace, forget it! You belong to me now.'

To reinforce the message, he pulled her against him and kissed her protesting mouth.

Outraged by his interrogation of Gran, she struggled to free herself, spreading her hands on his chest and using her full strength to push him away. It was like trying to budge a large rock. He held her fast with one arm, his other hand clamping her head, and went on kissing her whether she liked it or not.

Fran didn't want to respond. She tried to ignore the messages his mouth was sending to all her nerve centres. Her brain told her he had no right to force her into submission, but the primitive woman inside her was glad he was angry and jealous.

In the end she gave up resisting. As soon as he felt her yielding, Reid picked her up and carried her to their bed where he stopped controlling her by force. They made love as equal partners and eventually went to sleep in each other's arms, as if nothing had happened.

In the morning she woke to find a note for her on his pillow. It was only then she remembered that later today he was flying to Bonn for a conference with German financiers. He would be away two nights. They had decided there would be no point in her going with him as he would have no spare time. The note said: *Didn't want to wake you. Will try to call you tonight. R.*

No 'love'. No row of crosses or hearts.

Fran sighed and got up. She knew that last night's lovemaking hadn't resolved the underlying tension between them. Reid wasn't happy. She wasn't happy. But if there was a solution she didn't know what it was.

Rather than staying in London during Reid's absence, she was going to stay with her mother.

Mrs Turner looked well and cheerful. During their first conversation, it emerged that while Reid and Fran had been honeymooning, she had been invited to stay with Mrs Heatherley and had greatly enjoyed the visit. Later in the year Mrs H, as Daphne Turner called her, was coming to see her garden.

'What a difference between her and Reid's other grandmother,' she said. 'I didn't take to Lady K at all. I expect you'll be glad when you have a place of your own, dear.'

Although Reid rang up that night and the following night, their conversations were brief and businesslike. He might have been calling his sister, if he had had one.

When Fran sounded out her mother's feelings about Julian's father, it emerged that Mrs Turner had long had a soft spot for him and would have liked to re-employ him if he hadn't found himself another job and another place to live not long after the bankruptcy had forced her to let him go.

Fran decided to go and see Jack Wallace and drop a few heavy hints. She had no intention of doing it via Julian. Any contact with him would be sure to infuriate Reid.

What he didn't realise was that seeing Julian again had opened her eyes to the nature of her love for him. Although it had lasted much longer than a first love usually did, that was all it had been: an immature passion now replaced by another unrequited love.

When and how she had fallen in love with her husband, she wasn't sure. Perhaps she had known he was special the first time she saw him. Then, in the same way that, when she was using the Internet, she clicked on links to track down the information she wanted, there had been a series of moments when her feelings about him had changed and developed. Looking back, she could see the progression...the undiagnosed emotion mixed with her angry reaction to their first meeting...the strong response to their first physical contact...the buzz she had felt the day he met her at the station...the terror that he might fall off the cliff.

Until finally it had hit her. I love him. He is the man I would go to the ends of the earth with. He is the man I would die for.

The fear that he was incapable of returning those feelings made her deeply unhappy.

When Reid came back from Germany, he hadn't been in the house more than a quarter of an hour before he took her to bed. It was then she discovered the pain of making love while suppressing the words she longed to say. It was like hearing the music of a song without the lyric: incomplete.

Afterwards, Reid lifted himself on his elbows. 'You're addictive. After two nights without you I was beginning to feel withdrawal symptoms.'

She smiled, her fingers playing with the thick hair at the back of his head. 'Me too.'

But she knew all he meant was that he had become used to having regular sex, not that he had missed her in all the other ways that people who loved each other felt bereft when they were apart.

Later, when they were having dinner alone together, she told him about her visit to Jack Wallace and her hope that it might not be long before he and her mother got together.

Reid didn't ask if she had been in touch with Julian. He said, 'I hope they have the sense to give it a trial run before rushing into marriage. Living with someone else is a major adjustment at any age, but even more so at theirs.'

'I don't think Mum would like that.'

'You must try to persuade her it's the sensible thing to do.'

The remark made her feel that, despite what he'd said in the bedroom, he wasn't finding his own marriage as uncomplicated as he had expected it to be.

A fortnight later Fran acted on two decisions. She enrolled for a course in interior design starting in September and she went to see a gynaecologist for advice on birth control. Up to now Reid had taken care of that side of things, a spin-off from his life as a bachelor. Now it was time for her to take over the responsibility.

She told him about the course first. Instead of asking interested questions, he said, 'You'll probably be pregnant by then. It's time we started working on that.'

'I don't agree. I think we should wait a few years so that I can get a career going. It was you who said I should exercise my brain. This is the way I want to do it.'

'London's already overloaded with designers. If I wait much longer to have children, I shall be in my fifties before they're in their teens.' Reid's tone was abrupt to the verge of being angry.

His attitude sparked her temper. 'If that's so important to you, you should have bought yourself a wife when you were in your twenties,' she retorted impetuously.

'I…did..not…buy…you!' he roared at her.

The mask was off now, revealing a man whose temper matched hers, except that the rage in his eyes was mixed with fierce desire.

Before she had any idea what he meant to do, he had grabbed her by the waist, swung her bodily over his shoulder and was charging out of the room where they had been talking and up the staircase to their private quarters.

Fran was too dumbfounded to react. She had known he kept himself at a high peak of fitness, but she wouldn't have believed he could race up the stairs with her hanging over his back.

By the time he dumped her on their bed, she was red in the face, breathless and still speechless. What was there to say when the man you loved was in a towering fury and had reverted to caveman tactics?

She watched him tearing off his clothes, and felt her emotions changing, the primeval woman inside her responding to the beauty of the powerful male body emerging from the disguise imposed by convention. Without it, he ceased to be a civilised City gent and became the man who deep in her heart she knew she had always wanted; a man capable of defending her, fighting for her and, if he chose, mastering her.

But this time he didn't have to. When he sprang on the bed beside her, she only pretended to resist for the buzz of feeling herself pinioned. There were many things about him she didn't know, but one thing she knew by instinct. He could overpower her, but he would never hurt her. He would only be brutal with words, never with actions.

Their mouths met in an explosion of emotion. Fran slid her arms round his neck and immediately felt his rage melting away, leaving only the hunger to possess her. She gave herself to him with total abandon, trying to express with her body all that was locked in her heart, perhaps never to be spoken.

Next day, while he was at the bank, she drove down to see Mrs Heatherley. His grandmother welcomed her warmly, moments later detecting that something was wrong. Fran admitted there was, explaining her feeling that Reid might be regretting their precipitate marriage.

'What makes you think so?' asked his grandmother.

'Since we came back from our honeymoon I've felt him...distancing himself.'

'He has a very responsible and not altogether congenial job,' said Mrs Heatherley. 'Reid *is* a complex man and he doesn't find it easy to discuss his deepest feelings. Most men don't. Has he told you about his parents' separation?'

'Only sketchily.'

'Nirmila, my youngest daughter—it's a Nepalese name her father chose for her—should never have married Reid's father. He was years too old for her. It was an infatuation she quickly grew out of. When Reid was ten she met a man who *was* right for her. Reid loved both his parents and was terribly hurt by what he saw as her desertion. It coloured his attitude to the entire female sex. It didn't help that in his twenties he was very much targeted by women with an eye to the main chance. I was beginning to think he might never meet someone who loved him for himself. Then you came along and I knew he had finally found the right girl for him.'

'But I'm not sure I am,' Fran said uncomfortably.

She was strongly tempted to unburden herself, but was restrained by the feeling that Reid wouldn't like her revealing the real basis of their marriage.

Instead, she said, 'Would you let me stay here for a few days? I'll let Reid know that I'm safe but I won't tell him where I am. I think we need some time away from each other.'

If Mrs Heatherley thought this a curious request from a recently married bride, she didn't show her surprise, but said mildly, 'Of course you may stay. Your mother tells me you have a flair for interior decoration. There's a cottage in the grounds which I want to do up. Perhaps you can give me some ideas.'

Later, while Mrs Heatherley was busy in the garden,

Fran got out her laptop and composed a letter to e-mail to Reid. When she had sent it, she rang the house in Kensington and asked Curtis to tell her husband there was a message waiting for him.

Then she rang her mother and Shelley, telling them both that Reid would probably be getting in touch with them because she needed time to herself and was going away for a while. They were not to worry about her. She would keep in touch.

Inevitably, they both wanted to know what was going on but Fran refused to be drawn. When she had rung off, she reread the letter now reposing in the electronic mailbox on the laptop Reid kept for personal correspondence. She wondered how he would react when he read, *Reid: I am going away for a while. You needn't worry about me. I'll be in touch when I've made up my mind what to do. At the moment I feel I can't keep my side of our bargain. Whatever happens, I shall always be glad that you were my first lover. If only the rest of our relationship was as good as that side of it, we should have no problems. But we do and I'm not sure they're curable.*

She had signed the message *Francesca* because that was how he thought of her.

That evening she persuaded Mrs Heatherley to tell her everything she could remember about Reid's boyhood and early manhood. His grandmother needed little encouragement. She admitted that he was her favourite. The way she spoke of him sent Fran to bed filled with longing to break down the barrier between them.

But, lying awake most of the night, she had a dispiriting feeling that Reid's closely guarded heart might never become accessible to her.

Next day, although dying of curiosity to know if he had rung up her mother and sister, and how he had sounded, she disciplined herself not to call them.

Every time Mrs Heatherley's telephone rang, she expected it to be him, seeking counsel from the one person to whom he might unburden himself. But the calls were always from other people.

At increasingly frequent intervals she went to her room to see if he had left a 'Where are you?' message on her laptop. The Inbox remained obstinately empty.

On her second night at the manor, exhaustion sent her to sleep. She woke up no closer to knowing how to tackle the future than she had been when she arrived.

That afternoon, the two women were in the drawing room, discussing Fran's ideas for the cottage, when a black Jaguar came round the bend in the drive.

'Reid!' she exclaimed, in sudden panic.

'Don't worry, my dear. You don't have to see him if you don't want to,' the older woman said calmly.

'You talk to him first,' Fran appealed to her.

'By all means.' His grandmother bundled Fran through a jib-door she hadn't known was there. It led into a small ante-room lined with books and furnished with nothing but a table and chair.

Fran sat down, her hands tightly clenched on her lap, every nerve in her body in knots as she waited for Reid to arrive on the other side of the secret door she felt sure he must know about.

It wasn't long before she heard him greeting his grandmother. The sound of his deep resonant voice, clearly audible, through the door, sent a shiver through her.

'This is an unexpected pleasure,' she heard Mrs Heatherley say. 'Why isn't Francesca with you?'

His reply was curt. 'Because she's left me.'

'Oh, dear…I'm sorry to hear that. But I shouldn't worry too much. Most newly-weds have quarrels. With that lovely red hair, it's not surprising she has a temper and you can be very irritating at times, dearest boy. Why don't you ring her up and eat a little humble pie? I presume she's gone to her mother.'

'No, she's not there, or with her sister. I've no idea where she is…and I'm as worried as hell. I behaved like a skunk. It's not surprising she walked out.'

'Women are very forgiving. They'll put up with appalling treatment from men they're in love with. I'm sure whatever you did wasn't so very terrible.'

'It was…and she doesn't…doesn't love me, I mean. I'm afraid this is going to shock you but we married for mutual convenience. Love didn't enter into it…not then.'

This statement was followed by silence until Fran heard the old lady say, 'But that's changed now on your side, has it?'

'Yes…I'm crazy about her. It's funny…I never used to fall in love the way most guys do when they're young. Now I've got it so badly I can't sleep or concentrate on work. I feel I'm going crazy.'

'That's a very good thing, dear,' his grandmother answered serenely. 'To fall in love with your wife *after* you've married her is really much more sensible than doing it beforehand.'

'But Fran doesn't feel the same way. She was in love with someone else. She married me on the rebound.'

'I'm sure you can make her love you if you put your mind to it. As your generation says, you have a lot going for you. I don't want to make your head swell, but you are very attractive to women, Reid, and you're a nice man too. It's an unusual combination. So many charmers are not very likeable at rock-bottom.'

'I wasn't nice to Francesca the day before she left me. I was a swine to her.' His voice had the ring of deep contrition.

Fran had never heard him speak in that tone before but clearly his grandmother was one of the few people to whom he could talk without reserve.

'And there's something else,' he went on. 'I can't keep my side of the bargain. She married a London-based banker with a settled future. When we were in the Pyrenees, I realised I couldn't go on wasting my life at the bank. If Dad hadn't been seriously ill, I should have opted out years ago. It's late, but it's not too late to become a professional climber. It's something I have to do, Granny. Even for Francesca, I can't go on with this...this masquerade at Kennards.'

'I'm amazed you've stuck it out so long, dear. I always felt you were a square peg in a round hole. I think you'll be doing the right thing. If we're lucky enough to have a vocation, we should follow it for all we're worth.'

'Yes, but how many women can stand being married to a climber? You've been through it. You know what it's like.'

'Indeed I do.' Fran could visualise the wry smile that accompanied this remark. 'It's a combination of heaven and hell. But I've never, ever regretted marrying your grandfather. There are two kinds of men in this world. The steady, reliable, "safe" men who are generally rather dull dogs, and the adventurers. They aren't as easy to live with but they're a lot more exciting.'

There was another pause before Mrs Heatherley continued, 'You know this modern proverb "There's no such thing as a free lunch"?'

'Of course, but I hadn't thought of it as a proverb before.'

'Certainly it's a proverb and a very good one. Love is not a free lunch. It has its price like everything else in life. If Francesca loves you and wants the best for you, she will have to pay for that with periods of anxiety.'

'I couldn't ask that of her, it wouldn't be fair.'

'My dear Reid, you really should know by now that life is *not* fair. Anyway it's up to Francesca. Open your heart to her and see what she says.'

'I would if only I could find her. *Where the hell is she?*' He sounded distraught.

Fran sprang up and opened the door. 'I'm here!' She rushed across the room and flung herself into his arms. 'Oh, darling, I've missed you so badly.' She burst into tears and buried her face in his shoulder.

Reid's arms closed round her so tightly that she felt her ribs might snap. After a moment or two his vice-like grip relaxed slightly but not very much.

'Thank God you're safe,' he said hoarsely. 'I've been going mad with worry.'

'I'm sorry.' Lifting her face, she was astonished to see there were tears on his cheeks too. He was breathing as hard and unsteadily as she was, his strong face contorted with emotions she had never expected to see there, or had thought him capable of feeling.

'Don't ever do that to me again. I've been in hell...thinking of all the things that might have happened to you. I can't live without you, Franny.'

'Nor I without you,' she whispered, her eyes streaming.

'I'm going to leave you to sort things out in private,' said Mrs Heatherley quietly, on her way to the door.

When it had closed behind her, Fran said, 'If you really do love me, there's nothing to sort out. If you want to live in a hovel in Kathmandu, that's all right with me. I don't give a damn where we live as long as you love me as much as I love you. Even half as much would do,' she added, beginning to smile. 'Oh, dear, now my nose is running. Have you got a hanky?'

Reid produced one and gave it to her, wiping his own face with the back of his hand, his eyes devouring her as if he couldn't believe she had materialised and was half afraid she would vanish again.

She was still mopping her eyes when he tilted her chin and kissed her as if only by mouth-to-mouth contact could he make sure she was real.

They went on kissing for some time, not with passion but with relief and tenderness. Passion would kindle later. For the moment they were both suffering from shock. The strange thing was that she knew just how he was feeling and she knew he knew what she felt. Suddenly they were communicating on a different level from before. It was as if a private line had opened up with messages going in both directions.

'You would hate a hovel in Kathmandu…and so would I,' he said, smiling. 'Fortunately my grandfather set up a trust fund for my father, which I've inherited, and Dad did the same for me. Combined with my own investments, they mean I can afford to support you in whatever style you fancy. Personally, I favour that château in France you saw in my acquisitions file, but first things first. Are you sure…very sure you can cope with being a climber's wife? I shan't be doing it *all* the time, obviously. Most of the mountains I'd like to tackle are only accessible at certain times of year.'

Fran said, 'Not all climbers die young like your grandfather. Some of them live long lives. Far more people are killed on the roads than fall off mountains.'

'I might be away for weeks at times when you need me.'

'But when you come back, it will be like your grandmother said…heaven. Like it is now,' she added softly. 'What I don't understand is why you didn't tell me how you *really* felt. You're not somebody who's shy and unsure of himself.'

'No…not in the ordinary way. But when you fall in love, for the first time, at my age, with a girl who was so committed to another man that she resisted all the pressure to experiment with sex, it's not a situation you know how to cope with,' he said dryly. 'When we were on our honeymoon, for the first time in my life I knew what it would be like to be perfectly happy. I saw that, if you loved me, and if I didn't have to go back to

Kennards, the future would be perfect. I could do something about the bank, but I couldn't make you love me and I didn't feel it was right to renege on our deal.'

'Let's call the deal off and start again...as a love match,' she suggested, nestling against him.

A long time later there was a tap on the door. Fran wriggled herself off Reid's lap before he called, 'Come in.'

It was Mrs Heatherley with a tea tray. He sprang up to take it from her.

'Thank you, dear...on the table by the window. I thought freshly baked scones with whipped cream and last summer's raspberry jam might have a restorative effect. Emotional storms leave one terribly hungry, I seem to remember.' She gave them both loving looks. 'But all is well, now, I gather?'

'All is fantastically well...couldn't be better,' Reid told her, smiling.

'I'm so glad. I felt sure it would be. The first time I saw you together I knew you were right for each other. As time goes on, one develops an instinct...'

While they were devouring the scones, Mrs Heatherley said, 'I have an idea I want to discuss with you—' her eyes twinkled '—when your mouths are a little less full. This house is far too large for one person, and I need more help in the garden. Your mother feels the same way, Fran. We get on so well, she and I, that I'm contemplating inviting her to come and live here. The house would have to be converted into two self-contained parts and the garden divided as well. She would want to bring her favourite plants. What do you think?'

'I think it's an excellent plan,' said Reid. 'What do you think, pussykins?'

It was the first time he had ever used a pet name. She gave him a loving look.

'The only possible snag is that Mum has an admirer…a nice man who used to be our driver,' she explained to his grandmother.

'That needn't be an obstacle. Half this house would be plenty of room for the two of them and a nice man around the place is always an asset. Anyway I'll suggest it to her. Now I'll go and get the vegetables for supper and you two can make up a bed. Reid knows where the linen is kept. I should have what we call Aunt Prissy's Room. It gets the morning sun.'

That night, after eating an orchard-reared roast chicken with new potatoes, young carrots, buttered courgettes and fennel from the kitchen garden, they climbed into a four-poster bed made up with the crisp linen sheets of an earlier era, and made love…with the lyrics.

'God…I love you so much. How did I live without you all these years? Never run away from me again. Promise?'

'Cross my heart. Oh, it's so good to be able to say it aloud. I love you…I love you…I love you.'

While from somewhere below a clock chimed eleven, and the ancient floorboards and rafters made the night noises of an old house, they lay in each other's arms, planning a future quite different from what either of them had foreseen when they made their bargain.

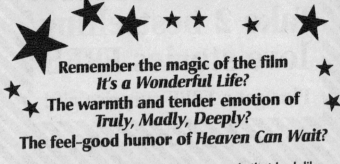

Remember the magic of the film
It's a Wonderful Life?
The warmth and tender emotion of
Truly, Madly, Deeply?
The feel-good humor of *Heaven Can Wait?*

Well, even if we can't promise you angels that look like Alan Rickman or Warren Beatty, starting in June in Harlequin Romance®, we can promise a brand-new miniseries: GUARDIAN ANGELS. Featuring all of your favorite ingredients for a perfect novel: great heroes, feisty heroines and a breathtaking romance—all with a celestial spin.

Look for Guardian Angels in:

June 1998: THE BOSS, THE BABY AND THE BRIDE (#3508)
by Day Leclaire

August 1998: HEAVENLY HUSBAND (#3516)
by Carolyn Greene

October 1998: A GROOM FOR GWEN (#3524)
by Jeanne Allan

December 1998: GABRIEL'S MISSION (#3532)
by Margaret Way

**Falling in love sometimes needs a little help
from above!**

Available wherever Harlequin books are sold.

Take 2 bestselling love stories FREE

Plus get a FREE surprise gift!

Special Limited-Time Offer

Mail to Harlequin Reader Service®

> 3010 Walden Avenue
> P.O. Box 1867
> Buffalo, N.Y. 14240-1867

YES! Please send me 2 free Harlequin Romance® novels and my free surprise gift. Then send me 6 brand-new novels every month, which I will receive months before they appear in bookstores. Bill me at the low price of $2.90 each plus 25¢ delivery and applicable sales tax if any*. That's the complete price, and a saving of over 10% off the cover prices—quite a bargain! I understand that accepting the books and gift places me under no obligation ever to buy any books. I can always return a shipment and cancel at any time. Even if I never buy another book from Harlequin, the 2 free books and the surprise gift are mine to keep forever.

116 HEN CH66

Name	(PLEASE PRINT)	
Address	Apt. No.	
City	State	Zip

This offer is limited to one order per household and not valid to present Harlequin Romance® subscribers. *Terms and prices are subject to change without notice. Sales tax applicable in N.Y.

UROM-98

©1990 Harlequin Enterprises Limited

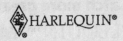

Not The Same Old Story!

Exciting, glamorous romance stories that take readers around the world.

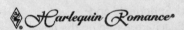
Sparkling, fresh and tender love stories that bring you pure romance.

Bold and adventurous—Temptation is strong women, bad boys, great sex!

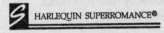
Provocative and realistic stories that celebrate life and love.

Contemporary fairy tales—where anything is possible and where dreams come true.

Heart-stopping, suspenseful adventures that combine the best of romance and mystery.

Humorous and romantic stories that capture the lighter side of love.

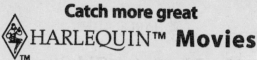

*The only way to be a bodyguard
is to stay as close as a lover...*

STAND BY ME

The relationship between bodyguard and client is always
close...sometimes too close for comfort. This September,
join in the adventure as three bodyguards, protecting three
very distracting and desirable charges, struggle not to cross
the line between business and pleasure.

STRONG ARMS OF THE LAW
by Dallas SCHULZE

NOT WITHOUT LOVE
by Roberta LEIGH

SOMETIMES A LADY
by Linda Randall WISDOM

*Sometimes danger makes
a strange bedfellow!*

Available September 1998 wherever
Harlequin and Silhouette books are sold.

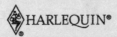 

Look us up on-line at: http://www.romance.net   PHBR998

MEN at WORK

All work and no play?
Not these men!

July 1998

MACKENZIE'S LADY by Dallas Schulze

Undercover agent Mackenzie Donahue's
lazy smile and deep blue eyes were his best
weapons. But after rescuing—and kissing!—
damsel in distress Holly Reynolds, how could
he betray her by spying on her brother?

August 1998

MISS LIZ'S PASSION by Sherryl Woods

Todd Lewis could put up a building with ease,
but quailed at the sight of a classroom! Still,
Liz Gentry, his son's teacher, was no battle-ax,
and soon Todd started planning some
extracurricular activities of his own....

September 1998

A CLASSIC ENCOUNTER
by Emilie Richards

Doctor Chris Matthews was intelligent, sexy
and *very* good with his hands—which made
him all the more dangerous to single mom
Lizette St. Hilaire. So how long could she
resist Chris's special brand of TLC?

Available at your favorite retail outlet!

MEN AT WORK™

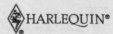